HIS LADY
BOSTON DOMS BOOK FIVE

JANE HENRY
MAISY ARCHER

Published by Blushing Books
An Imprint of
ABCD Graphics and Design, Inc.
A Virginia Corporation
977 Seminole Trail #233
Charlottesville, VA 22901

©2019
All rights reserved.

No part of the book may be reproduced or transmitted in any form or by any means, electronic or mechanical, including photocopying, recording, or by any information storage and retrieval system, without permission in writing from the publisher. The trademark Blushing Books is pending in the US Patent and Trademark Office.

Jane Henry and Maisy Archer
His Lady

EBook ISBN: 978-1-61258-185-9
Print ISBN: 978-1-64563-163-7
v1

Cover Art by ABCD Graphics & Design
This book contains fantasy themes appropriate for mature readers only. Nothing in this book should be interpreted as Blushing Books' or the author's advocating any non-consensual sexual activity.

CHAPTER 1

"Blake! Yes, baby. God, *yes*! Just like that. I'm so *close!*"

This information was not a surprise. Blake had every ounce of his considerable focus trained on the woman who was currently riding him. He'd seen how her eyes, potent and dark as black coffee, had widened, and how her creamy skin had flushed a deep pink, all the way from the graceful arch of her cheekbones down to the rosy-tipped breasts that brushed his chest each time she took him deep inside her. And it was not a minute too soon—he could feel his own orgasm ready to overtake him, his balls tightening in a way that said this one was going to be bigger than anything he'd ever felt before. The taste of her on his tongue was like a fucking aphrodisiac, and he couldn't hold out for long. Patience was *not* one of his virtues.

But first he had to take her over one more time.

"Find it, angel," he ordered, his fingers digging into her lush backside to hold her in place as he pistoned his hips up beneath her. "I want you to use your fingers and take yourself there."

She braced one hand against his shoulder, levering herself up, while the other trailed over his chest, across the hard, chiseled plane of his abs, and down to the place where they were joined. Her beautiful eyes went unfocused.

Christ Jesus.

"That's it, gorgeous. Touch yourself. I want to watch," he growled. "I want to hear you when you come apart and scream my name."

Her eyes cleared for a moment and met his.

"You want an awful lot of things," she teased breathlessly, even as her fingers found her clit and began to circle in perfect counterpoint to the rhythm he'd set. Her eyes stayed locked on his, and her lips—those fucking pillowy lips that he'd been picturing wrapped around his dick for-fucking-*ever*—clamped shut as she fought to stay quiet, to stay in control, to deny his command, to *defy him*.

That would never do.

"You're gonna give it to me," he told her, his voice sounding like sandpaper even to his own ears. "I *own* your screams, just like I own this sweet pussy. Just like I own the rest of you."

Her eyes met his—hot with challenge and begging him to prove his dominance, just the way he liked it—and she rode him harder, her even white teeth sinking into her bottom lip as she stayed stubbornly silent.

Blake smiled. God, but this woman—*his* woman—was perfect for him.

"Tell me," he demanded. "Tell me that you belong to me."

He lifted his hand to one bobbing breast and cupped it, his fingers toying with her. She whimpered and clenched her eyes shut, while the fingers at her core moved faster and faster.

"If you wanna come, you're gonna do what I tell you, *young lady*."

Her pussy clenched around him as his words drove her higher, just as he'd known they would. *Young lady.* Old enough to be legal, but young enough to turn heads. Young enough that if the world ever saw his hands on her body, the way his callused fingers tweaked her nipple, they'd be appalled. They'd call him a lecher, an old man who'd knowingly corrupted a sweet young thing.

And they'd be right.

She was more than that, of course. Not *just* a young lady, but *his* lady, his lover and partner. But it was also no less than the truth, and the taboo of it sent a shudder through her body that made his dick impossibly harder.

"What if I don't wanna say it?" she moaned, testing him… testing them *both.*

The fingers tugging her nipple tightened to the point of pain and he stilled beneath her.

Her mouth and eyes flew open with a startled "Ah!" She glimpsed his face, and whatever she saw there made her shake her head desperately. "Oh, no! No fair! You can't just *stop!*"

She moved both hands to his stomach and pushed against him, trying to gain leverage, to slide herself more firmly down his cock, but he easily captured one of her wrists in each of his hands, and clamped them against her hips, holding her immobile.

"Seriously, Blake! You can't just stop like this!" she cried. "It'll hurt you as much as me!"

He snorted, but didn't bother to reply. It would very likely hurt him *more* and they both recognized it. Nevertheless, she knew very well that he could and would stop, even though it would take every particle of the self-control that he'd honed over decades as a soldier and as a dominant to keep him from thrusting up into her wet heat.

Their eyes held, kindled—her will battling against his—until finally, inevitably, she swallowed, and the tension bled from her body. One side of her mouth kicked up in the lopsided smile that he loved, and she gave him the words he craved.

"*You* own me," she said, low and serious like a vow. "*You* own me, Blake."

"Fuck yes, I do," he snarled. "You're *mine.*"

His hands released hers, only to clamp her hips tighter, holding her at just the right angle for his thrusts while their eyes remained locked. One pump, then two... that was all it took. She threw back her head and her long black hair tumbled behind her, the feathery ends brushing the tops of his thighs as she came and came and *came...* screaming his name the entire time.

He eased her through it, though his heart was thundering in his chest, until her last tremors had subsided. Then he planted himself firmly inside her, wrapped his arms tight around her, and flipped them so that she was on her back beneath him. He lifted her leg higher, planting her knee against her chest, and began to stroke, faster and faster, lost to the sensation of being inside the woman he loved and the soft clench of her body as he moved against her.

"Mine," he repeated. "Mine. Mine. *Mine.*"

∼

MOTHERFUCKER. Not again.

Blake threw himself from the bed as though it were on fire. His mind was a haze of lust and confusion, his chest was tight, his dick was hard enough to break rock, and his balls ached like he'd just been practicing his kickboxing without his fucking cup.

Jesus. A dream. Another goddamned dream, and he'd woken himself up with the sound of his own voice calling out. Disgust settled like a lead weight in his gut, cooling the worst of his arousal... but not taking it away completely. Nothing seemed to do *that* anymore.

He braced a hand on the tall chest of drawers near the bed and breathed deep. *In-two-three-four. Hold-two-three-four. Out-two-three-four. Hold-two-three-four.* He imagined what the recruits he'd trained back in the day would say if they could see their Master Gunny using the combat breathing techniques he'd taught them to keep his shit together after a stupid sex dream.

He clenched the hand he'd braced on the dresser into a fist and felt a reluctant tug of amusement. He *was* in combat, in a way. A battle of the wills. Master Gunnery Sergeant-turned club owner Blake Coleman versus… his own damn self.

His eyes lifted to meet his own reflection in the mirror. God, but he looked tired. Tired and *old*, with every one of his nearly fifty-five years showing plainly on his face. There were dark smudges beneath his eyes, and the silver-streaked brown hair he usually kept ruthlessly tidy was now tousled and wild. Out of his control, like so many things in his life had been from the moment he'd learned that his wife, Josie, had cancer a year and a half ago, through her death three months later, and every damn day since. But no longer.

This is the end, he promised his reflection. *No. More.*

Grief was a part of life. He wasn't fool enough to believe a man could escape it through strength of will, and he hadn't tried. He'd railed, he'd cried, he'd bargained. He'd stepped back from his friends. He'd loosened the reins at The Club, the BDSM mecca he owned and operated just a stone's throw from Fenway Park, and allowed his trusted friends and employees to take on more responsibility. But he'd be damned if he would allow his own *mind* to turn traitor on him, to make him dream in glorious fucking detail about shit that he should never be contemplating, about a woman who was wrong for him on every level.

Unacceptable. It was time to get a handle on this.

He scrubbed his forehead with his free hand, rubbing the sleep from his eyes.

When he opened them a moment later, he caught sight of the framed pictures which had been arranged just-so on the top of the dresser, first by Josie, and then by their cleaning lady, Consuela, who had started coming once a week when Josie got too sick to keep the house as pristine as she liked it.

"Keep Consuela on after I'm gone," Josie had begged. "You'll need someone to take care of you, at least for a while."

Her concern was baseless, if you considered that he'd enlisted in the Marines the day he'd turned eighteen and had spent years doing his own cooking, cleaning, and laundry. He was perfectly capable of taking care of himself.

But Josie hadn't wanted him to have to. Blake had learned early on in their marriage that Josie delighted in taking care of him, both as his wife and as his submissive.

So when her tired eyes had grown round and alarmed at the idea of him managing the place on his own—maybe picturing him suffocating under the weight of a decade's worth of dust—he'd agreed to keep Consuela on, and he hadn't had the heart to change his mind in the months that had passed since Josie's death.

Without conscious thought, his hand snagged the picture frame and dragged it closer, so that he could inspect it in the milky, pre-dawn light.

It was an image he'd seen a thousand times before—him in his uniform, hair high and tight, fresh back from a stint in Saudi Arabia during the first Gulf War, not even thirty years old and cocky as hell. Josie in her puffy dress, all white satin and lace, with her blonde curls fluffed out to the nth degree and looking for all the world like the twenty-year-old virgin she was. He was looking straight at the camera, ready to take on whatever life threw at them. She was looking at *him*, awestruck, like he'd hung the moon.

A familiar pang twisted his stomach.

Their marriage had been a good one. They'd never been able to have kids, but that hadn't seemed to bother Josie much once the initial disappointment faded. She'd instead found her calling in studying and researching dominance and submission, and mentoring others in the D/s community through her blog, SubHaven. And Blake... well, he'd opened The Club.

He ran his thumb over the smooth wood of the picture frame. A quarter of a century had passed since that day. Sometimes it felt like yesterday. Sometimes he could barely remember who he'd been back then.

His mind tripped to Slay and Matteo, Diego, Paul, Donnie, Dom and Tony, the younger men—all dominants, like him—who he considered the core members of The Club. He considered all of them friends, despite the fact that all of them were currently around the age he'd been when the picture was taken.

He snorted. In a lot of ways, those guys were further along than he'd been at their ages, not that he'd ever admit it out loud. But back then he hadn't even known what BDSM *was*. He'd thought he'd have to subdue the protective, dominant qualities that had served him so well in the military for the sake of his marriage.

If it hadn't been for Josie, he might never have known better.

She'd been the one who'd read the romance novels, the one who'd gotten the idea that his natural leadership and her natural submissiveness could become something *more*. She was the one who'd approached him, encouraged him to talk with other dominants, introduced him to the concept of chat rooms back when the internet was in its infancy. It had opened his eyes to what their marriage could be, what *he* could be, and allowed him to fulfill his potential in so many ways.

He owed Josie, huge. And he always would.

He straightened, and the brush of his soft flannel pajama pants against his still-hard cock made him shudder.

Fuck.

He owed Josie, and this was how he repaid her? Humping the bed like a teenager with a wet dream? Having completely inappropriate fantasies about a woman who was decidedly *not* his wife, and who was… who was…

He slammed the flat of his hand on the dresser top, then spun around and stalked down the hall to the kitchen, ignoring the way his cock tented his pants. The whole situation was intolerable, and it was up to him to fix it.

He reached the kitchen and went through the motions of fixing himself a cup of coffee, while his mind turned over the problem.

Issue number one: he had gone too long without sex. He waited for guilt or shame to rear its head as he acknowledged this fact, but neither did. He had a sex drive, a *strong* one, and always had. Sex was a biological need for him, a simple fact of life. He'd done the deed exactly six times since Josie had passed, and each time he'd been slightly less uncomfortable, feeling less like he was cheating. Every other time he'd gotten off, which was to say, every morning and most evenings, he'd relied on his own damn hand, and that was because of...

Issue number two. Ironic as it might seem given that he spent nearly all his waking hours in a club that catered to many people who were willing and eager for no-strings sexual gratification, those offers didn't apply to him. He wasn't just a *member* of The Club, or even an *employee* of The Club. He was the owner. The man who sat behind the video monitors and ensured that everyone stayed safe, sane, and consensual. A father figure to some, a mentor to others, Big Brother to the rest. Essential, but... apart. He needed a partner who understood his need for dominance, but wasn't in awe of him. And that brought him to...

Issue number three, which was thornier. Because ultimately, he didn't *only* need sex. No-strings sex and spankings were like cotton candy to a starving man. They were tasty, and they temporarily took the edge off, but they completely lacked substance. Blake wasn't a boy, and hadn't been for a long time. He was a *man*, and he knew exactly what he wanted and needed—a woman who would submit to him, a woman he could nurture and protect. He didn't need a new wife, he didn't need a life-long commitment, but he needed permanence. *That* was what his mind and soul craved. And it was *that* lack that was sending his mind off the rails right now.

It was the only explanation he could fathom for why he was fantasizing about the least-submissive, least-appropriate, most-annoying woman in the Greater Boston area, Elena Slater.

There was a time, shortly after they first met, when he'd found her charming. Cute, even. Her confidence, her bright humor, and her unquenchable curiosity had been a welcome distraction during Josie's illness, and Elena's experience as a nurse had given her the rare ability to express sympathy without pity, even during the hardest days.

But over the past few months, he'd ceased to look at her as a potential submissive who needed mentoring, and the confidence and curiosity he'd once found adorable had become infuriating.

"It's just a simple question," she'd complain defiantly, after asking her thousandth question about Shibari, or spanking implements, or consensual non-consent. With each progressive question, his explanations became briefer, less comprehensive, until he'd finally glared at her in frustration and reminded her of something she'd once told him—that she was a twenty-something woman with an Internet connection. If she wanted information, for the love of fuck, she could look it up. That way, when her big brother, Alexander "Slay" Slater, Blake's right-hand man at The Club and trusted friend, got pissed off that his baby sister was becoming a walking, talking kink encyclopedia, he could blame the folks at Google and not invite Blake's ass to the mat to settle his beef UFC-style.

He ran a hand over the hard ridges of his abs, feeling the muscles he'd honed through years of intense, dedicated workouts, and took a cautious sip of the scalding hot coffee.

Not that he couldn't hold his own against Slay, of course. Slay was taller and younger, but didn't have a fraction of Blake's experience. The issue was that you could hardly fight a man when you felt like he had a point, and Blake didn't want Elena discussing that shit with him any more than Slay did. She was nearly thirty years younger than he was, for God's sake. His friend's baby sister.

Or maybe you want to discuss it too *much?*

His mind helpfully called up an image of Elena as she'd been in his dream, her hair a black halo around her gorgeous face, her dark eyes on him as she took his cock. He definitely hadn't been thinking of her age when she…

Blake took another deep gulp of the coffee, grateful for the way it scorched his mouth and pulled his thoughts back to the present.

His hand tightened around the mug until he worried that it might crack.

She's too young. She's Slay's sister. She's not the type of submissive you need.

His cock twitched in his pants, calling him a liar, and he growled as he dumped the remainder of the coffee down the drain.

He needed to find himself a new sub. But first, he needed to get reacquainted with his fucking hand in the shower.

THIRTY MINUTES LATER, Blake was clean and in a clearer frame of mind. He shoved his feet into his sneakers, and grabbed his phone from the charger, ready to head out to his favorite Crossfit box and all-out *attack* the workout of the day. Despite the momentary relief he'd felt in the shower, frustrated arousal still thrummed within him, and he was going to burn it off in the easiest outlet available to him—the gym.

But one quick glance at his phone screen had him stopping in his tracks, sinking down onto the worn leather couch in his living room as he cradled the device in his hands.

Such a simple thing—a new email reminding him to renew the domain name for the SubHaven website—and just like that, a pang of grief and remorse caught him square in the chest.

SubHaven, the blog Josie had started years and years ago, had been more than his late wife's hobby, it had been Josie's passion, creative outlet, and social connection. He'd stayed out of it, beyond knowing the basics and occasionally reading posts when she asked him to, since his involvement seemed to make her self-conscious, but she'd always made sure he knew her passwords, just in case. And in the fifteen months since Josie had died… and the months of illness before that… had he thought about using them? No. Not even once. Not even to write a quick post to let the regulars know what had happened. Not even to wish them all farewell.

Shit.

He stuck the phone in his pocket, made his way to the back bedroom that Josie had used as an office, and fired up her computer. The machine began to purr almost immediately, the monitor blinking to life in a flood of white light, and Blake smiled even as he shook his head. His own damn computer at The Club started up with a noise like a fucking lawnmower, as cranky and slow as his grandma when her arthritis had flared, but Josie had had a way with technology. Taught herself everything she needed to know and then some—enough to help Slay and Matteo when they needed help with their off-books security gigs, and enough to build her own system from the ground up. He wished he'd taken the time to learn more about it from her before...

He sucked in a breath and shut the thought down.

The system booted with her blog front and center, opened to the last thing she'd posted. Without thought, he sat his ass in Josie's rolling chair and scooted it closer to the screen, reading the words she'd written.

It was an open reply to a letter, something Josie did fairly often when she got a communication from a dom or sub and thought the answer would benefit the entire community. He knew that she worked hard to craft those posts, thinking about them for days and sometimes weeks, wordsmithing and fine-tuning until her message was clear. She knew that her words impacted her readers, and she felt an overwhelming responsibility to get things "right."

In this case, the letter was from a newbie submissive with the screen name LanieLove. He found his lips curving up in a reluctant smile as he read her letter.

Hi, LadyHaven - I'm a twenty-six-year-old woman who's a professional and part-time student. I've been fascinated by D/s for the longest time, and every word I read on your blog convinces me more and more that this is something I'd like to try... but I haven't the foggiest idea how to turn the fantasy into reality! How does your average girl find herself a dominant? Billionaire control-freaks and obsessive vampires are pretty thin on the ground around here. Do I coat myself in liquid latex and march into a club? Play Russian roulette in the online chat rooms and hope I don't wind up with a serial killer? And even if I do find a guy who wants that kind of a relationship, how do you submit to a person you barely know? How do you know when it's safe to give another person control?

Josie's reply had been straightforward and informative, recommending some groups that might have local chapters while stressing the standard *safe, sane, consensual* motto, but the last paragraph caught his attention...

If there is one other piece of advice that I could give you, LanieLove, one that I wish I'd had when I was at your stage of the journey, it's to remember that the dominants you've met on the pages of your latest romance or on the big screen—the millionaire, mind-reading, super-hero doms that make us drool and sigh—do not exist. No pre-packaged "perfect" dominant lies waiting for you to find him. And LanieLove, you shouldn't want there to be! A true D/s relationship is a bond that grows and deepens over time as you develop trust and understanding until you get to the place where you need to be. And it doesn't matter how much experience each partner has had in the lifestyle, because D/s has as many incarnations as there are dominants and submissives, and every partnership will find the balance that works for them. And Lanie, when you and your partner find the one that works for you, it's more beautiful than anything you've ever seen or read about. Beware of anyone who expects you to change yourself to fit their ideals without taking your needs and goals into account. D/s is not one-size-fits-all. Educate yourself (I'm always happy to answer your questions!). Communicate with your partner or potential partner. Keep an open mind, but be safe.

He sucked in a deep breath and ran his hand over his jaw, feeling a weight he hadn't known he was carrying break free. She'd been happy in their marriage, his Josie had. It was right there in the words she'd written.

He'd known it on a certain level, of course, because he'd worked to make it so. Submission had seemed to come as easy as breathing to Josie, and their relationship had been calm and comfortable. He'd never had reason to question it.

But recently, watching as the men around him found their soulmates—each couple enduring their own trials by fire and working their way through them, he'd started to wonder if maybe, just maybe, he and Josie had been missing something. Had he lost his focus? Taken his eye off the ball? Could he have amped things up a bit further, taken things a bit higher, knocked them out of their comfort zone and into something even deeper, even *better*?

Reading her reply reassured him that, whatever questions *he* might have on that score, Josie hadn't had any.

He absentmindedly scrolled down the page and saw a private reply from LanieLove, and another from Josie, who suggested switching their conversation to email instead. Curious, he opened Josie's email program.

Jesus. There were over two *thousand* unread messages in her inbox, some of them from as recently as this week, asking for her help or advice.

Another deep breath had him closing the program and beginning to type his first—and last—post on SubHaven. A post he titled simply, "An Update."

With a sigh, he hit Publish a few minutes later, and rolled himself back from the desk. Sometime—like next week or next month or next year—maybe he'd come back and wade through that email backlog, but he wasn't in a hurry. They wanted *Josie's* advice, after all, not his. For now, he had a date with an assault bike at the gym.

But just as he reached over to touch the power button on the monitor, the system dinged an alert and a chat screen opened—someone trying to chat with Josie.

He tamped down a flare of annoyance—hadn't he *just* explained that SubHaven would be shutting down?—and went to close the screen, when he saw that the sender was LanieLove. Curiosity had him reading her message.

LanieLove: I'm not sure if anyone will get this. I just wanted to say that I'm so sorry to hear this news. LadyHaven was a treasure and she's been missed.

His hands hovered over the keys, debating how to reply, or whether he should even bother, but something compelled him to type.

LadyHaven: Thank you. That's kind of you to say. I know my wife gained as much from the blog as her readers did. She considered you friends.

The sight of his reply under his wife's username startled him, but before he could debate switching, he received a reply.

LanieLove: I felt the same. I didn't know her for very long—we only messaged back and forth for a few months—but I felt like she was my partner in crime.

The notion of sweet, sensible Josie being anyone's partner in crime made his eyebrow lift, though there was no one there to see it.

LadyHaven: Crime? Really?

LanieLove: Er. Not crime, exactly.

LadyHaven: Relieved to hear it.

LanieLove: Ha! More like matchmaking. She was helping me find a dominant.

LadyHaven: Ah, yes. One who wasn't a billionaire or a vampire?

A long pause followed, so long that he wondered whether she was going to reply, but then she did.

LanieLove: You read that?

LadyHaven: Of course. LadyHaven posted your letter, along with her reply. Surely she got your permission first?

LanieLove: Oh. Yes, she did. It's just... I guess I didn't expect that any DOMINANTS would read it.

He laughed out loud.

LadyHaven: You didn't know that at least a third of the readers of the blog are dominants?

LanieLove: Crap. I guess I hadn't really thought about it. Maybe I should have been a little less sassy, huh? Guess this solves the mystery of why I haven't found a dom, even after a year of looking?

LadyHaven: Well, as a dominant, I can tell you that having a sense of humor is a point in your favor. Your letter made me smile, and I didn't think that was possible this morning.

LanieLove: Bad day?

LadyHaven: Considering the sun hasn't fully risen in this time zone, it's too early to tell, but it was shaping up that way.

LanieLove: I can imagine. I have a friend who lost his wife recently and... well, it's changed him. I guess it's to be expected, but...

LadyHaven: But you're worried about him?

LanieLove: Kinda, yeah. He doesn't talk anymore, never jokes around. He's the strongest guy I've ever met, but he's gotta be hurting. I wish he'd let someone in.

Blake stared at the flashing cursor on the screen for a long moment, then finally typed words he'd only recently discovered to be true.

LadyHaven: Give him some time. Sometimes it's easier to just retreat from the world. He'll know when it's time for him to start living again. You can't rush it.

LanieLove: That's good advice. How about you? Have you started living again?

Blake sucked in a breath. Had he? Honesty compelled him to reply.

LadyHaven: I'm getting there, Lanie.

LanieLove: I am so glad. I know LadyHaven would want that for you.

Before he could formulate a response, let alone type one, another message followed.

LanieLove: Listen, I know we don't know each other at all, but... If you're having a bad day, please reach out. I can't help my friend, but I'd like to know that I could be there for SOMEONE, you know? And sometimes it's easier to talk to a stranger, I think. Or if it's weird to talk to me, talk to your friends. Humans are herd animals, after all.

LadyHaven: Herd animals?

LanieLove: Seriously! I read it in a psychology magazine at my dentist's office.

LadyHaven: Well, then it must be true.

LanieLove: LOL. It just means we're not meant to go it alone!

He read her message and felt his lips curve, then without allowing himself to think too deeply about it, he typed.

LadyHaven: I'll keep in touch.

LanieLove: You will?

LadyHaven: Yes. Because LadyHaven would want me to make sure you found yourself a dominant who'll treat you right.

LanieLove: Aw. That's sweet. I haven't found anyone I think she'd approve of yet. LadyH had VERY high standards for a dominant.

Blake snickered.

LadyHaven: Well, thank you. That's quite a compliment.

LanieLove: Pardon?

LanieLove: Oh, my gosh! I hadn't meant YOU!! I meant for ME.

LanieLove: I mean, not that she didn't have high standards for herself, too.

LanieLove: Obviously!

Her messages flashed on the screen in quick succession and her embarrassment had him chuckling.

LadyHaven: I know what you meant.

LanieLove: Okay, good!

LanieLove: Hey, I've gotta go in a minute, but I'll send you my phone number in case you want to message me when I'm not logged in to chat.

Blake's eyes widened, even as her phone number appeared on his screen. He felt his shoulders tense with shock and displeasure.

LadyHaven: Please tell me you did not just do that.

LanieLove: Do what?

LadyHaven: Share your phone number with a TOTAL STRANGER online!

LanieLove: Oh. You're not a stranger, though. You're MisterHaven.

Blake felt his teeth grinding together and didn't stop to consider why he felt so unreasonably concerned with the welfare of a person he'd only exchanged a few words with.

LadyHaven: You seem like an intelligent woman, Lanie, so think about this... How the hell do you know who I am? I could be an ax murderer. I could be planning to scam you out of money, trace your phone to find your location, anything!

LanieLove: That's crazy. You're not the CIA, and it's just my phone number!

LadyHaven: And what happens when I reverse-search your phone number, LanieLove? What if I spend $20 and run an identity check? Then what?

Frankly, Blake wasn't exactly sure what information a search like that *would* net for him—this was much more in Josie's wheelhouse than his own. But he was confident there was a wealth of information out there for someone more knowledgeable and less honest than him, and this girl, whoever she was, needed to be careful.

LanieLove: Oh.

Blake snorted. *Oh?* That was her response?

LadyHaven: Be smart, Lanie.

Her reply was a long time coming, and when it did, it was two simple words.

LanieLove: Okay. Sorry.

Blake waited for more, noting that the green light next to her name was still lit, showing that she was still online, but nothing else came.

He regretted that their easy back-and-forth had ended that way —it had been a long time since he'd smiled as much as he had in this one random conversation, and he'd honestly planned to check in with her and mentor her if he could—but it was worth the sacrifice if she learned her lesson and stayed safe. He reached out to flip off the monitor again.

Once again, her message chimed through just before he hit the button.

LanieLove: I've gotta say, if you're an ax murderer, you're a pretty shitty one. LOL. Next time, don't give away the whole plan, MisterH! Gotta get back to work, but text me if you want to.

And then the green light next to her name went out.

He sat for a moment staring at the screen and shaking his head. Part of him wanted to end this here and now, but another part of him recognized that this—a sweet, uncomplicated, mentoring relationship—might be exactly what he needed. If nothing else, it would distract him from the woman who'd been haunting his dreams.

He grabbed his phone, and plugged in Lanie's number, then sent her a simple one-word message:

Brat.

He found himself looking forward to her reply in a way he hadn't looked forward to anything recently. He shoved himself to his feet, stuck the phone in his pocket, and headed out to the gym, only vaguely aware that he was whistling while he did it.

CHAPTER 2

*E*lena absentmindedly picked up the glass Alice handed to her, thanked her with a distracted nod, and took a sip. She practically spit it out, sputtering and coughing, as she flagged Alice down.

"Alice, what is this shit?" she asked, her nose wrinkled in disgust, slamming the traitorous glass on the small table. She was sitting in the main bar at The Club, her friend Hillary on her left and Hillary's boyfriend Matteo on the right. Hillary, a small, pixie-like blonde, widened her eyes at Elena's reaction. Matteo, Hillary's large, tattooed, Italian boyfriend, feigned a cough, covering up a snort of laughter. Elena frowned as her brother Alex—known here at The Club as *Slay*—pulled a chair out, turned it around, and straddled it.

"That, baby sister, is called a Shirley Temple," he said with a frown. "Otherwise known as The Drink that Girls who Drive Themselves Home After Hours get after they've had two mixed drinks." His eyes narrowed, his brow furrowed at her. "And if I'd seen you order the second, you'd have been drinking ginger ale with fancy fucking cherries after the *first*."

Elena threw up her hands in disgust. "For crying out loud, Alex! Are you for real?"

Hillary's brows shot up as she daintily wiped her mouth with a cocktail napkin. "He's for real, honey. And anyway, don't feel so bad. You get used to the virgin cocktails after a while."

It had only been seven months since Hillary had had her first baby, and tonight they were having a bit of a reunion. Hillary took a sip of her beer. "God, that's good," she breathed. "It's been way too long."

Elena frowned at her. "Thanks, babe. Rub it in, why don'tcha?"

Since Alice, the waitress serving drinks, was Slay's girlfriend, Elena was screwed. And part of her knew he was right anyway. If any of the girls who came to her at *Centered,* the women's center where she volunteered, asked her how many drinks were enough, she'd have firmly told them never to drive under the influence, and to exercise caution when drinking, but part of her rebelled against being *told* what to do. Five years her senior, Slay had always been her protector, and even though she was now twenty-seven years old, he still hovered like some overgrown masculine version of a mother hen.

It was only in recent months Elena had taken to coming to The Club anyway, and she wondered for the umpteenth time why she didn't just pack it up and go hang with her girls somewhere else. In the Hub of Downtown Boston, there was no shortage of places to go. But here, at The Club, she'd made friends with Alex's buddies— Hillary and Matteo, Matteo's twin brother Dominic and his wife Heidi, and their younger brother Tony and his girlfriend Tessa. They were awesome people, all into mild kink that totally pushed Elena's buttons, and if Elena really had to admit the truth, she sorta liked that coming to The Club was safe. She was protected, and didn't have to worry about losers hitting on her. No one would think to harm a hair on Alexander Slater's sister's head, though his protection had a certain downside. She hadn't been approached by a guy since she stepped foot in The Club.

"Elena, for God's sake, how many times do I have to tell you not to park your car on the street?" growled a familiar, gritty, pissed-off voice. Elena reached for the fucking useless Shirley Temple, and grimaced as she took a pull of the virgin drink.

"Why, hello there Blake," she said with mock-pleasantness as he approached their table. She saluted him with a cherry skewered with a toothpick, grinning her most charming smile as he glowered at her, and then popped the cherry in her mouth, crunching it between her teeth.

Blake, owner of The Club, stood a few feet away, dark blue eyes boring into hers. His dark beard was fuller as of late, peppered with silvery gray that matched the silver at his temples and accentuated the blue of his eyes. A tall man, muscular and well built, he was the stern, protective, father figure of the group, *Master* Blake to all who worked there. Tonight he wore a button-down blue shirt stretched across his massive chest, and well-worn jeans that hugged his hips, upon which his hands now anchored as he glared.

Blake had been the grumpy sort even *before* he'd lost his wife, but since she'd passed, he'd been a veritable bear.

Needs to get laid, Elena thought to herself, hiding a smirk. "Cool your jets, Oscar the Grouch," Elena muttered. "You know I like to park on the street because I don't *belong* in the employee parking lot, and unless you want to hire me, I have no plans on parking where I don't belong."

She met his gaze unflinchingly, ignoring how Alex stiffened, Hillary drew in breath, and Matteo snickered. This was about her and Blake, and she wasn't gonna cave. People did not *talk back* to Master Blake. Even Slay, who deferred to *no one*, looked up to him as his mentor.

"Elena," Slay warned, as Blake's eyes narrowed.

"You should hire her," Matteo said, taking a swig of his beer. "Honest to God, she'd make a kickass domme. You ever tied a guy up, Elena?"

Elena grinned, and tapped her glass to Matteo's beer. "Pulling out the red stilettos and leather mini skirt tonight, Matt," she said. "Why didn't I ever think of that?"

"Stereotype much?" Hillary said with a giggle, but Slay and Blake were unmoved.

Elena took another sip of her sweet drink, and met Blake's eyes. "What do you say, old man? Wanna take me on? Hire me as Dungeon Mistress? Ever fancy being tied up by a woman in stilettos? I'm sure I could swing a mean whip. Hell, it might even help you loosen up a bit."

Hillary choked on her drink, Matteo coughed again, while Slay marched to her side and Blake's eyes narrowed.

"You're lucky she's your sister, Slater," Blake growled. "I make it a rule never to mingle with guests, but so help me God, if she wasn't your sister, I'd spank her impertinent little ass 'til she couldn't sit for a week." Slay had reached Elena's side and squeezed her shoulder in warning.

"Normally, I'd tell any guy who wanted to lay hands on her to take a fucking leap," Slay growled. "But Jesus, Blake, I'm about ready to hold her down for you myself."

Elena rolled her eyes. "Shaking in my boots," she muttered, as she watched Blake turn on his heel and storm off. She ignored the pulsing between her legs, and wished she could blame the heat that rose in her chest on the alcohol. Given that it was nothing but sugar and ice, there was only one thing she *could* blame, and he'd just stormed off to his office. With a scowl, she grabbed Slay's beer bottle and took a pull, earning a heated glare, before handing it back. Time to go home.

ELENA STOOD TO LEAVE, giving her brother a quick hug. Matteo led Hillary to the back, to check his hours before they took off, while Alex walked with her to the exit, when his phone buzzed.

"Gotta take this," he said, putting the phone up to his ear. "You good?"

Elena rolled her eyes. "I can cross the street by myself, Alex," she said with a sigh.

He narrowed his eyes at her, shaking his head, but turned his attention to the phone in his hand, as she made her way to the exit. She didn't even have a buzz going, *thankyouverymuch*, and was not looking forward to the evening ahead. Her regional certification testing was due the following Saturday, and she was knee-deep in reviewing for the major exam. The material she had to review was always incredibly boring. Her everyday work as a labor and delivery nurse kept her up-to-date with the practices she needed to know, but the details of more recent procedures were still vague. She'd have several hours of studying to put in that night, followed by a full shift at the hospital starting at seven a.m. the next day, and then a solid shift of volunteering at *Centered* the following afternoon. She sighed. Her one free night had gone off with a veritable bang.

The bouncer opened the enormous steel exit door with a nod, and Elena slipped past. Her stomach growled in hunger as she made her way to her car, reminding her that she hadn't eaten dinner. She sighed as she clicked the button on her key ring to disengage her car alarm, and then jumped as the lights flicked on, revealing a dark figure leaning up against the hood of her car. She straightened her shoulders, holding her keys the way she'd been trained at the safety seminar at work, finger above the panic button so that if anyone made a move, she could hit the alarm and hopefully scare them away. But having grown up on the streets of New York City, she could defend herself if necessary, and was not afraid of confrontation.

Who was that big guy leaning up against her car? And why *her* car? But as she drew near, she exhaled in relief. The familiar stark blue eyes met hers in the dim glow from the streetlights.

"Elena."

"Blake," she said with a nod. Though part of her longed to call him what the others at the Club did—*Master* Blake (what would it be *like* to call someone *master?*)—she couldn't quite bring herself to say the words. "What's up?" she asked, unlocking the car, yanking open the passenger door, and putting her purse on the seat. His brows shot up.

"Tell me you don't drive through the streets of Boston with your bag on the passenger seat," he said, a look somewhere between sternness and shock crossing his features.

She blinked. "Okay. I don't drive through the streets of Boston with my bag on the passenger seat."

He frowned. "For real?"

She let out a breath of exasperation. "Um, I do, yes. How else can I reach what I need at the lights?"

He growled. "A girl like you, growing up with Slater in New York City, and you don't know better than to leave your bag where anyone can just reach in and grab it?"

She shrugged. "I lock my door."

He raised a brow.

"Look, did you just come out here to give me shit about where I place my bag and where I park again? Or did you have another purpose?"

He pushed himself to standing, his brows furrowed. The chill spring air made her shiver. She wondered briefly if it were just the cold that made her shiver, then quickly discarded the notion as he stepped closer. "I just wanted to apologize. I came on really strong in there and shouldn't have said what I did."

She rolled her eyes. "Fine. Fair enough. Come out to apologize, and get on my case. Great." Even as she talked, she wanted to stop herself, close her mouth, shake her own shoulders. What was it about this infuriating man that brought out the bitch in her? She sighed. "But I'm not sure what you're apologizing for."

He stepped closer to her. She could smell the faint scent of him, strong and masculine, woodsy and clean. His hands were on his hips, and he watched her with his piercing blue eyes as he neared, the blue making his rugged face younger-looking. They were hypnotizing. Her breath caught in her throat. He was much larger up close than she'd remembered, and for the umpteenth time, she rued the day that her older brother got every one of the "Slater enormity" genes. Though she stood as tall as she could, she was still slight in stature, and had to fairly crane her neck to look up to Blake.

Blake cleared his throat. Was he… nervous? Or was it something else?

They were so close now she could see the flecks in his deep blue eyes, the wrinkles on either side indicating a man of experience, humor, and emotion. Her eyes traveled down, taking in the wide expanse of his shoulders, the triangle of white t-shirt at the very top of his blue button-down, the way his jeans hugged his hips, his shirt tucked into his trim waist. Her breath caught. *Way to go, Elena. Gawk like a fucking schoolgirl.*

Jesus, the boys she'd dated in college suddenly seemed… *juvenile.*

Damn, why did she have to feel intimidated? She was used to alpha males, having been practically raised by her brother, king of the alphas himself. Though her father had been a certifiable asshole, she'd spent her entire childhood around Alex and his gritty, fearless friends, then later his Marine buddies. She was no stranger to men who were larger than life. So why did Blake make her nervous? She tossed her chin, grateful for the protection of the swath of long, black hair that swung in front and momentarily blurred her vision.

He cleared his throat. "I wanted to apologize for saying I'd spank your ass."

A nervous laughed bubbled up, covering the heat that rose to her chest and the pounding of her heart. *Fuck,* the words *spanking your ass* in that deep, gritty voice of his did wonderful, terrible things to her body. The very *idea* of Blake holding her over his lap sent delicious shivers down her spine. Her eyes fell on the wide leather belt at his hips. She swallowed with effort.

Elena had to play it off, or she would lose whatever footing she had with him. "Whatever," she said, with a shake of her head. "You know Alex would kick your ass if you laid a finger on me. But anyway, I don't come here because you have awesome chicken fingers even though *you do*, or because your fucking Shirley Temples are so delicious *which they are not*. I come here because I like the people, and the kink turns me on." She shrugged a shoulder. "So. Go ahead, tell me you'll spank my ass. I'm hardly going to report you to Feminists R' Us or anything. I know you're full of shit anyway."

The second the words left her mouth, she wanted to take them back. His eyes darkened, his jaw clenched, and she could feel the heat of his eyes focus on her. She swallowed, ashamed of herself, as he took another step toward her.

"Am I?" he said, his voice impossibly deeper, challenging, and her mind played out the scene. He would grab her by the wrist, spin her around, and bend her over his knee…

She swallowed. "Of course," she whispered, meeting the challenge in his eyes as she lifted her chin defiantly. "I know you're all talk, old man."

Why did she feel the need to drive the barb home? His eyes flickered a moment before he responded.

"Old man?" he said, stepping so close now she looked up at him, so close she could almost taste him and *fuck* she wanted to. "You're right," he said in a low growl. "I *am* an old man." His voice was low and edgy, a deep rumble she felt in her toes. "I'm old enough to be your father. You'll do well to remember that."

Why the fuck did he have to go and ruin everything?

"You're nothing like my father," she hissed.

His brow furrowed. "Didn't say I was," he retorted.

God, what a dumbass. Why did she say anything at *all*? She cleared her throat.

"Well, thank you, I *think*, for whatever it is you came out here for, but I need to get home. While I'm at it, I'll drive recklessly through the streets of Boston with my purse on prominent display." She shoved past him, suddenly pissed at him, wanting to tell him to fuck the hell off.

She heard him behind her now, as he stalked back to The Club. "Sure thing," he said. "You have a good night, Elena," he said, his voice dripping with sarcasm.

And with that, he was gone.

SHE BERATED herself all the way to the intersection right before she got home. Alex would be pissed at the way she'd bitched at Blake. Blake was someone he looked up to, and there was no one in the entire world she loved more than her brother. It was with great reluctance that Alex allowed her to go to The Club to begin with, with no small thanks to Alice pleading for her. "With you, and all of us there, there's no place safer in Boston than The Club," she'd told Alex, and it was a good point.

Alex had reluctantly agreed, though he was still ridiculously over-cautious. It had taken six months before he'd okayed her going past the front part of The Club where everyone met, and getting more than a passing glance at the main bar, or the "big kids' table," Alice called it. (Of course, Elena wasn't alone in this. Alice had told Elena how Slay had made *her* work the front for months before *she'd* finally gained access to the real part of The Club, where all the action happened, too.) It had taken another six months before Elena had finally taken part in a scene, and only because Alex hadn't been on for that night, and Matteo had been acting as Dungeon Master. Slay had just about flipped his lid when he found out she was engaging in scenes, and they'd had an epic throwdown. Fortunately, she'd emerged the decided victor, mostly because of Alice going to bat for her *again*. "You can't discourage her from looking into the lifestyle the very people she spends time with eat, breathe, and sleep." Again, a good point.

Elena picked up her phone from where it sat on the passenger seat, noting with childlike glee that she'd gotten her way with the over-the-top protective Blake. *Dangerous, my ass*, she thought, then realized she was silently telling off a man who was miles away, and shook her head. She hit speed-dial, hoping to catch Alice on a break, but it went to her voice mail. She sighed, tossing the phone back on the seat. She needed to talk to someone. Someone who would listen and understand.

Picking her phone up again, she went for the second number on speed-dial, Hillary's sister Heidi, another member of The Club, submissive to her husband Dom. In the past year, as Elena had gotten to know Heidi, she'd been grateful for her friendship. She was the only one in the group who was married, and Elena admired the depth of her relationship with her husband. She'd been submissive to him from the very beginning, and the two of them positively doted on each other. Elena was drawn to them, as she wanted what they had so deeply, and Heidi, being older than Elena and more experienced in so many ways, felt like a big sister.

Heidi picked up on the second ring. "Hello?"

"Hey, Heidi," Elena said, pulling to a stop at a red light.

"Elena! How's it going, honey?"

Elena felt sudden tears blur her vision, and she blinked them angrily away. God, was she hormonal or something? Why did the tenderness in Heidi's voice make her want to cry?

"Hey," she said, hiding her emotion with forced cheerfulness. "Just wanted to call and say hi. Haven't seen you guys for a while and I'm about to settle in for a night of thrilling studying."

"It's nice to hear your voice," Heidi said. "I've missed you! And gosh, I can't believe your exam is this Saturday. How's the—"

A loud wail came on the other side of the phone. Elena had completely forgotten Heidi and Dom were babysitting for Matteo and Hillary's baby, Francesca. "Ohh, poor baby," Heidi's muffled voice said on the other side of the phone. "Dom, did she hurt herself?" She came back to the phone, snickering. "Uncle Dom tried to play peek-a-boo and apparently got a little carried away. The baby's crying like she's just seen the boogeyman."

Elena giggled as the wails increased in volume and Heidi's voice grew distant as she tried to help her husband. "Honey, why don't you hand her to me, and I'll see if I can settle her down for bed?"

Heidi sighed, coming back on the phone. "I'm sorry, Elena. Francesca's getting really tired, and I think it's time I get her to bed. I can't really talk now. Are you okay, honey?"

"Oh, I'm fine!" Elena lied. "Of course, do what you need to do. Maybe we can catch up soon?"

"I'd like that," Heidi said warmly. "Why don't you come over for dinner this week?"

"My schedule's *crazy*," Elena said, truly not able to even come up with an hour of free time in which she could swing by Heidi and Dom's. "But I'll stay in touch and we can connect after the big exam? Sound good?"

"Yes! You have a good night," Heidi said, and the two of them disconnected.

Elena tossed the phone on the seat, and frowned, suddenly feeling odd man out. Heidi and Dom had each other, and so did Hillary and Matteo. Alex and Alice were damn near inseparable. The girls at work were good friends, but everyone was busy, and it seemed everyone she *knew* was with a partner. She just needed to *talk* to someone.

As she pulled into the parking spot outside her apartment building, hope fluttered in her chest.

Maybe she'd be able to catch MisterHaven online. Maybe he'd be free. She'd had at least a brief chat with him every day this week, and was starting to really like him.

She'd been a regular reader on LadyHaven's blog, and had gotten to know MisterHaven through the eyes of his wife. Although she'd never met LadyHaven, she'd felt as if she were a friend. It was through LadyHaven's blog she'd come to know about dominance and submission to begin with. She'd known Alex was a dominant, but had only thought of it as some sort of sexual kink, and given that he was her brother, she was more than happy to leave the details of *that* alone. But she'd stumbled across the blog, and the way LadyHaven wrote, Elena was drawn to it. Over the years, she'd never missed a post. It had been like losing a real friend when LadyHaven had passed away. She knew if the two of them had been able to meet in real life, they'd have been close friends.

At first, she reached out to MisterHaven because she'd wanted to comfort him. It was hard enough for a husband to bury his wife. How much harder would it be for a dominant? A man who had not only loved and cared for his wife, but devoted himself to the daily meeting of her needs? There was something decidedly different about the intimacy between the couples she knew at The Club. It was somehow deeper, more connected, and she suspected, after several long online conversations with LadyHaven, that when a dominant or submissive in a long-term relationship lost a partner, a part of themselves actually died a little. For a brief moment, she thought of Blake, and how difficult it was losing his Josie, but she quickly brought herself back to the present.

Elena glanced at the clock and groaned. She *had* to get her studying in before it got much later. She would make herself something to eat, then pop on just for a few minutes. She sat at her laptop and booted it up, grinning when a flashing blue message bubble popped up on her screen. Though MisterHaven had her cell phone number, he'd told her he wanted to get to know her a little bit better before he used it.

MisterHaven: Hey. Just saying hi. How are you tonight?

She smiled and typed a response. He'd finally figured out how to change his screen name.

LanieLove: Hey. Just getting in before I settle down for a night of studying. Are you still there?

A few second later, a response popped up.

MisterHaven: Still here. ::waves hand::
Elena grinned.
LanieLove: Okay, give me five.
MisterHaven: Say please.
She bit her lip at the tease, feeling the latent command.
LanieLove: Give me five, PLEASE.
MisterHaven: No need to yell. Okay, wish granted.

She got up quickly, put her phone to charge on the base, and walked to the kitchen, her footsteps light. MisterHaven had been a dominant for *decades,* and she knew that it was more than friendship that drew her to him. His intrinsic desire to lead and protect came across in every interaction. The way he spoke of his late wife made Elena sigh like a lovesick teenager reading a heartfelt romance. The love between LadyHaven and MisterHaven had been beautiful and lasting, the stuff dreams were made of.

She opened the fridge and frowned. There was a half-wilted head of lettuce, a small Pyrex container of leftover enchiladas, and sundry other totally useless condiments and leftovers. Damn. She sighed, regretting not having grabbed something to eat at The Club or a drive-thru before heading home. Shutting the door to the fridge, she turned to her cabinets. They had little more to offer than her fridge had. She opened a nearly-empty jar of peanut butter, but put it back when she realized she was out of bread and crackers, finally settling on a foil-wrapped package of strawberry Pop-tarts.

She grabbed it, along with a can of soda and a bar of chocolate, her stomach now gnawing with hunger. Opening her laptop back up, she glanced at the time. Shit. Her foraging through the kitchen had taken nearly fifteen minutes.

LanieLove: Still there, MisterHaven?
MisterHaven: Still here. That was much longer than five minutes, though.

She could hear the reproach in his tone, and her heart hammered in her chest. Though they were only friends, he was an exacting man, as she well knew from both their interactions and having read LadyHaven's blog.

LanieLove: Sorry about that. I had trouble finding something to eat. I'm starving.

MisterHaven: Why did you have trouble finding something to eat?

LanieLove: I haven't gone grocery shopping, and there's hardly anything here. I settled on a gourmet package of Pop-tarts, chocolate, and soda. At least the sugar will help me get through studying tonight.

MisterHaven: Are you serious?

She paused and eyed the screen nervously, suddenly embarrassed.

LanieLove: Um, yes?

MisterHaven: Sweetheart, you'll crash with all that sugar. Nothing else to balance all those simple carbs isn't good for you.

Elena's pride stabbed at her and her response flew from her fingers before she could retract.

LanieLove: Thanks, MisterH, but I didn't ask your opinion. I don't need you to father me.

There was a pause and no response came on her screen. God, had she scared him away? Great. Just *great*. She needed a friend to talk to, and she'd gone ahead and chased off the only one who was even around. And did she have to be so snarky to this good, honest, dependable man who still mourned the loss of his wife?

Maybe Blake was right. Maybe she *did* need a spanking. Tears pricked the back of her eyes, just as a response came on the screen.

MisterHaven: I think it's time you and I had a straight talk, Lanie.

Her fingers shook nervously as she replied.

LanieLove: Yes, sir.

Her eyes widened, as she fruitlessly tried to hit the backspace. It was too late. She'd already hit the "send" button. Yes, *sir?* What the actual hell? In her *entire life* she'd never called a man *sir*, and MisterHaven was not her dominant. She groaned out loud. What had gotten into her? But to her relief, he rolled with it and didn't comment.

MisterHaven: Lanie, you know I am a dominant. As such, I can't help but look out for your needs. Now, I don't really know you, and you don't really know me. But I see a sweet girl, who was a friend to my wife when my wife really needed a friend. That means something to me, Lanie. It means a real lot to me.

Elena's eyes filled with tears that she didn't bother to swipe away, as he continued. She missed LadyHaven so much it made her cry. How much harder was it for him?

MisterHaven: I like you. You're a good girl. You brighten my day with your humor and honesty. But I see you as a girl with no keeper, and it's against everything in me not to speak up when I see you doing something that might harm you. I can't help but look out for you, because I've been doing this since before you were even born.

She felt the sincerity in his words, the concern and even the sadness, as she quietly cried and read his messages.

MisterHaven: Still there, honey?

LanieLove: Yes, sir.

This time, she did not regret the term of respect. It felt almost natural.

MisterHaven: So I'm not going to apologize for looking out for you. In fact, I fully intend on continuing to do so. Is this something that you are going to be able to handle? Because although I am not your dominant, and I won't require your obedience to me, I also won't tolerate disrespect.

She closed her eyes, a fresh sob escaping. She was so very grateful he was where he couldn't see her, as she'd hate for him to see her losing her shit over something so simple as the fact that he fucking *cared* about her.

LanieLove: MisterHaven, I understand. And I'm sorry. Please forgive me.

MisterHaven: There's nothing to forgive, honey. We just needed to have this talk. Are you okay?

Elena wiped her eyes again before she responded.

LanieLove: I am. It's just... I'm tired. It's been a really long week and it's going to get even more intense.

MisterHaven: I understand. So tonight, you have to study, and then tomorrow you've got to work?

LanieLove: Yes. I have about three hours of studying to do tonight, after I eat my super healthy dinner.

MisterHaven: lol. Okay. Listen, this is what I want you to do. Pull up your to-do list.

LanieLove: Ummm...

MisterHaven: Start one, kiddo.

She grinned, pulling up the note app on her phone.

LanieLove: Done.

MisterHaven: On your list, write "make a grocery list." When you wake up tomorrow, I want you writing out your list and stocking up on easy, but healthy snacks to get you through this week. Okay?

LanieLove: Got it. She took a minute and did what he said.

MisterHaven: Now, as much as I'd love to spend the night chatting with you, you have studying to do, and you need to get a good night's sleep. So for now, let's call it a night. Set a timer on your phone and when the timer goes off, you get yourself to bed. No watching TV or cruising Facebook. Get yourself ready for bed, and get the sleep you need. Got it?

She frowned, but saw the wisdom in his instructions. How did he know she spent hours unwinding binge-watching Netflix, then dragging herself through her shift at the hospital fueled by Starbucks and vending machines?

LanieLove: Okay. If you say so.

MisterHaven: I do say so. I'm going to wish you good night, and send you a good night kiss you can put on your cheek for being a good girl. Okay?

God, how sweet was that? She swallowed, and even though she knew it was silly, she didn't even care. She reached out a hand, grabbed a fistful of air, and smacked it on her cheek grinning.

LanieLove: Thank you. Sending you a big ol' hug back around your bossy neck.

MisterHaven: Perfect. You do what I said, and let's check in tomorrow morning. Good night, honey.

LanieLove: Good night, MisterHaven.

She saw the chat screen go dark. She sat staring at the screen in front of her for a moment, before she shut her laptop, and stretched. It was an odd relationship; unlike anything she'd ever experienced. He didn't hit on her, like the guys she'd dated in the past had. Did he even flirt? Even when he called her *honey* or *sweetheart* it didn't feel like flirting. It felt… nice. Protective. Caring.

She shook her head. He'd given her instructions, and oddly, she felt invigorated with the knowledge. Someone cared enough about her to give her the direction she needed. She frowned as she pulled open her study books and sat cross-legged on the couch. Why did she *need* someone to give her direction? Wasn't she capable of handling things on her own? Glancing at the empty foil-wrapper on her desk, she gave a self-deprecating snort. Whatever. She'd been so busy at work, studying, and volunteering that she really hadn't taken care of herself the way she needed to. And wasn't that the beauty of being friends with a dominant? He could give her the little bit of guidance she needed, and maybe, just maybe, having someone to watch over met his own needs.

Yeah. That's all this was. He needed someone to boss around, so she'd humor him for a bit. Couldn't hurt. He was really only looking out for her.

She clicked her pen open, and opened her study book.

CHAPTER 3

"Hey, boss, can I talk to you?"

"Yep. Hang on." Blake glanced over the numbers on the screen in front of him once more, verifying their accuracy, then clicked save, before turning his attention to the woman who stood in his doorway.

His secretary, Daphne, had her hand braced on the doorframe, and was holding a sheaf of papers, an uncharacteristic look of annoyance on her pretty face. Daphne had worked at The Club for a few years, handling memberships, room reservations, and all the other public interactions that Blake had neither the time nor the patience to handle. She was one of the few trusted employees he'd leaned on more and more over the past year. Tall and willowy, with her pale skin framed by a waist-length curtain of red-blonde hair, she reminded Blake of an innocent maiden he'd seen in a painting once… at least until she opened her mouth. Daphne cursed like a sailor, handled business negotiations with the ruthlessness of a battle-seasoned general, and was the first person to jump in with an inappropriate comment or dirty joke anytime a situation got too tense, but she did it all while wearing a smile that could light up a room. That smile was missing tonight.

"Problem?" Blake surmised, nodding toward the papers in her hand.

Daphne hesitated, looking at Blake's face while chewing her lip. "Er… maybe. But you know what? Lemme talk to Matt about this, rather than bother you with it."

Blake's eyes narrowed. "Pardon?"

"Well, I… I know you're really busy, and you've been pretty stressed, and I don't wanna burden you when I could just bug Matt or Slay."

"Bug Matt with what?" Matteo asked, popping his head in from the hallway behind her. The former soldier's broad shoulders seemed to take up the entire doorway, and as always, there was a light of mischief just beneath the surface of his green eyes. He gave Blake a chin lift in greeting and turned his attention to Daphne.

"Oh, good! We can talk at my desk!" Daphne said eagerly, ushering Matt back into the hall with a gentle shove. Over her shoulder, she called out, "Sorry to have bothered you, Blake."

God, had things gotten that bad? Had he retreated to the point where his people thought he shouldn't be bothered with the day-to-day running of his own business? *Shit.*

"Daphne!" Blake barked in a warning tone. When her head reappeared in the doorway, he pointed at one of the chairs in front of his desk. "Sit. And Matteo, I need you to hear this too."

Without another word, Daphne sat, though she still looked wary. Matteo, his curiosity piqued, came into the office, but chose to lean against the far wall, instead.

"I know I've been a bit preoccupied over the past few months," Blake told them. "I needed to sort my shit. I needed to grieve for my wife. And I am grateful—more than I can express—that all of you, particularly the two of you and Slay, were there to pick up the slack for me. But it's time I stopped going through the motions and started really living again." He remembered his conversation with LanieLove and felt his lips twitch into a smile.

"It's time," he repeated. "And this is *my* club. So, when you have a problem, you don't hesitate. You come directly to me. Both of you. And make sure that gets circulated to every other member of the team. We're back to business as usual. Understood?"

Despite his unfiltered words and harsh tone, Daff's face lit up. "Yeah! I mean, *yes,* Master Blake. Understood."

One corner of Matt's mouth lifted in a smile, and he gave a single nod. "Understood."

Blake nodded once, closing that conversation hopefully forever, then gestured towards the papers Daphne held. "So?"

"Right! Okay, so…" Daphne's face grew serious as she laid her stack of papers out on the desk. "We've had an influx of crazy emails."

Blake glanced briefly at the papers, and then back to Daphne. "This is nothing new, Daff. Crackpots have been condemning us to hell since the day we set this place up. If they're not trying to save my soul, they're offering me some way to lose weight or enlarge my penis."

Blake could *hear* Matteo sucking in a breath, but before he could make the joke that Blake *knew* had to be hovering on his lips, Blake continued, "I believe you should forward all of *those* offers to Master Angelico's inbox."

Matteo snorted and Blake chuckled silently to himself.

Daphne made a strangled noise that was halfway between a cough and a laugh, then continued, "Right, boss. Will do. No, I know we get those emails on a regular basis. But these are different. For one thing, all of the messages are from the same group." She leaned forward in her seat and pointed to the paper. "They call themselves The Church of the Highest Prophet."

Blake and Matteo exchanged a glance. "The Church of the Highest Prophet?" Blake repeated. He felt an inexplicable clench in his gut as he said the words, some sixth sense that told him this wasn't like the harmless emails he'd gotten in the past. "I've never heard of them."

Daphne nodded. "Neither had I, and that's because they're fairly new. Just opened about a year ago, according to their website."

"They have a website?" Matt asked.

Daff rolled her eyes. "*Everyone* has a website, Matteo."

Matt pushed off the wall and prowled over to the desk for a closer look. "Simmer down, Daffy. Just an observation." His voice was mild but firm.

Daphne sighed. "Yes, they have a website," she confirmed in a more pleasant tone. "And if their propaganda is accurate, they have a membership of over 10,000 people."

Blake leaned back and whistled through his teeth. That was a high membership for a church that had started mere months ago. "And now they're targeting us? Spamming our inbox?"

"Sure seems that way," Daphne said. "I started noticing the name of the church maybe six or seven months back. We'd get one or two emails a day, and I'd click delete, and that would be that."

Blake nodded. That was the stand they'd always taken when it came to weirdoes and scammers. Ignoring attention-seekers was the best revenge.

"But then, maybe a month ago, the number of emails started increasing. It went from a couple to a couple of *dozen*, almost overnight. And over the past week or so, it's been more like a couple of hundred."

"A couple of *hundred*?" Blake repeated. "Every *day*?"

Daphne nodded. "And even *that* wouldn't be such a big deal in and of itself. I set up a filter that sends any email mentioning the church to its own box, so I can go through and delete them later, without having their spam clogging my inbox. But when I clicked on a couple today, I saw these."

Blake and Matteo leaned forward to look at the paper Daphne placed on top of the stack. It was a picture—a grainy, unfocused, black-and-white image that seemed to be taken by an old-school security camera, but the subject was clear: The Club. The photograph clearly showed the exterior door to the bar area on the first floor, as well as the street number—826—emblazoned on the awning above it. Below it was the caption, *The devil hides his lair in plain sight!*

Blake sighed. The location of The Club was hardly a secret—with hundreds of regular members and even more guests, it would be impossible to keep the location under wraps. Still, the street address wasn't something they advertised, either, if only to protect their members from idiots like the members of this so-called church. They were going to have to beef up security. *Shit.*

"Shit," Matteo sighed, echoing Blake's thoughts. "We'll need to double security tonight."

"Uh, guys?" Daphne said.

Blake nodded at Matteo. "Inside *and* outside. We'll need to consider hiring a couple of the guys Slay works with, maybe bring them on board as contractors."

Matt nodded. "On it."

"Guys?" Daphne said again.

"And I'll give a heads up to all of the wait staff to be alert for anything unusual," Blake said. "We'll handle it."

Daphne waved a hand in the air impatiently. "Guys!" Blake brought his eyes to hers and she continued, "You haven't seen the worst."

She flipped the first page over and showed them a second image. Another photograph, this one darker, though more detailed.

"Cell phone camera," Blake murmured, and caught Matteo nodding in agreement. "*Fuck.*"

The shot had been taken at night and from a distance. A man stood on the street with his arms folded, his hair gilded by the glow of a streetlight, his face tilted down and scowling. Though it was impossible to make out the details of his surroundings, his identity was clear.

It was Blake, himself.

And the caption read, *The devil walks among us.*

"They're coming after you *personally?*" Matteo asked, his voice heavy with disbelief and anger. "Blasting your picture out there, for any nut job with a God complex to see? Jesus."

Blake clenched his jaw, and blinked against the red fog that clouded his vision. Without conscious thought, his hands curled into fists.

"Show me the email," he demanded.

Daphne gazed at him, and whatever she saw in his face made her eyes widen when they met his. "Uh. Maybe…"

"*Now.*"

Daff swallowed, and grabbed a third sheet of paper from the bottom of the stack, placing it on top.

It was a forwarded copy of a letter that The *fucking* Church of the *fucking* Highest Prophet had sent to the idiots they called their "flock," and reading it did nothing to dispel Blake's rage.

It is with a heavy heart that I must inform you that our sinful neighbors at The Club, the devil's own lair, continue to promote immoral behavior and licentious acts within their walls. They have not heard our pleas. They have ignored our gentle entreaties to repent. They have refused to heed our warnings.

The time for words has ended. The time for action has begun.

The Club has been a blight on our community for too long. We must rid ourselves of this diseased limb by any means necessary, to ensure the safety of our children and families. It is our duty to ensure that our friends, our neighbors, and our public servants are aware of this evil, before its poison spreads further. I encourage each of you to contact your elected representatives. Let them know we will no longer peacefully accept this scourge on our city!

"Motherfucker," Blake said, flinging the paper across the desk to land in front of Matteo. "Get a load of that doomsday shit."

Matt read quickly and blew out a breath. "Jesus. That's fucked up."

Blake turned to Daphne. "I need every email from these assholes copied into a folder on the network. Access only to you, me, Matt, and Slay."

Daphne nodded, and hurried out of the room.

"I want to know *everything* about this '*Church*,' " Blake told Matt. "What kind of money do they have? Where do they get it? Where are they located? Who is their leadership?"

Matt nodded, "I'm working the floor tonight, but I'll tell the guys…"

Blake shook his head. "No, not the guys. *You*, Matt. You and Slay. Call Donnie and ask him to cover the floor. There is no higher priority than this right now."

Matteo nodded once again, but his brow creased. "Boss, I admit they're saying some scary-ass shit here. I don't blame you for being freaked if you feel like you're being targeted. We'll deal with this ASAP, but we don't need to go off the deep end."

Blake braced his hands on the desktop and pushed himself up to a standing position, so that his eyes were on a level with Matt's. "We are not discussing this. We are not debating this. *No higher priority*, Matteo. Yeah?"

Matteo blinked twice, obviously taken aback by Blake's intensity. His eyebrow raised and curiosity swirled in his eyes, but his jaw firmed. "Yeah, Blake. Sure. No higher priority."

Blake nodded once, then sat back down and turned toward his computer. "Let me know as soon as you find something."

Matt took this as the dismissal it was, and left. The moment the door closed behind him, Blake pushed his chair back and grabbed the picture off his desk to study it further. Once again, the image made his gut churn.

No doubt Matteo thought Blake was losing his shit, that grief had turned him into some kind of cowering pussy who wanted to protect his identity at all costs. The idea was almost enough to make Blake laugh.

Almost.

In truth, Blake couldn't care less if they took a picture of him. What Matteo didn't know, *couldn't* know, was that the identity he needed to protect was not his *own*, but that of the person hovering just outside of the camera lens—the woman he'd been scowling at so viciously just a few nights ago, as she stood in the street and rolled her eyes at his concern for her safety.

Elena Slater.

He laid the picture down and leaned back in his chair, folding his hands against the hard, flat plane of his abs, which he'd tortured just that morning in the gym, and sighed, considering his options. He could call Elena himself, tell her to stay away from The Club until they'd learned whether the "church" was just a bunch of crazy spammers or something more sinister, but he knew the crazy, stubborn female wouldn't listen. In fact, he admitted, she was just stubborn enough to insist on coming, loathe to show the slightest bit of weakness. He felt a spurt of amusement and something like... *pride*, before he quashed it.

She'd also take great delight in defying him just to see him riled, he reminded himself. She was a pain in the ass, that's what she was.

His other option was to call in reinforcements.

He tapped a button on his phone and was rewarded with Daphne's immediate, "Yes, boss?"

"Call Slay for me. Ask him to stop by before he leaves."

"You've got it!" she chirped.

Blake and Slay were similar in a lot of ways, and he knew that once Slay was aware of a potential security issue, he'd make sure Elena stayed away from The Club. Blake couldn't help the grin that slid over his face as he imagined Elena's reaction when Slay told her. Nor could he help the brief surge of possessiveness that followed, the instinctive knowledge that *he*, Blake, should be the one to protect her, to lay down the law to keep her safe.

He scrubbed a hand through his hair, and willed his cock to deflate, but the fucker didn't listen. His cock seemed to be attuned to the slightest suggestion of Elena- the smell of her perfume, the memory of her voice, the sight of her lips, the sound of her name.

No matter that he worked out twice daily now – doing Crossfit or weight training every morning, running five miles every evening—he couldn't exhaust himself enough to prevent his mind from conjuring her while he was sleeping. Every night, she haunted him. Sometimes in his dreams, he claimed her right here at The Club, sprawled out face-down on a spanking bench with her hands tied and her ass bright-red from his ministrations. Sometimes he took her slowly, almost reverently, with his tongue owning her mouth the way his cock owned her pussy. One memorable time, he'd awoken to find he'd been dreaming of throwing her over this desk, right here, while the air was heavy with the sweet smell of her arousal and her voice cried out "Master Blake" loud enough for the entire building to hear.

It was a good thing Slay would soon ban her from The Club, he thought, as he adjusted himself beneath his desk. The Elena who screamed his name so prettily was nothing but a fantasy. The real Elena didn't want his help, his guidance, or his protection. She'd proven that the other night.

Old man.

He sucked in a sharp breath against the urge to show her just how *young* he could be, where she was concerned.

His phone chimed in his back pocket and he grabbed it, his annoyance with Elena and his worry about the harassing emails dissipating immediately as he saw that he had a message from LanieLove.

LanieLove: Guess who aced their exam today?

Blake smiled.

MisterHaven: Hmmm... How many guesses do I get?

LanieLove: lol! Nevermind, meanie. WE DID IT!

MisterHaven: That's wonderful. I'm so glad, honey! Great job.

LanieLove: Thanks! And I'm sharing this victory with you. If it hadn't been for you talking me off the ledge, forcing me to make a to-do list and get things under control, I would've been too messed up to focus. So thank you, bossypants. 😊

Blake felt something loosen inside him, but for once, he didn't bother analyzing it.

MisterHaven: You're very welcome. And you know, those good habits weren't temporary. You need to keep going with that to-do list, and I'm going to be checking in to make sure. Okay?

LanieLove: Yes, sir.

Blake grinned. She'd fallen into the habit of calling him sir without any prompting whatsoever. A natural submissive if he'd ever met one.

MisterHaven: Okay, good. So, how are you celebrating?

LanieLove: Like a mature adult! Working.

MisterHaven: Tonight?

LanieLove: Yep. And tomorrow night, too. One of the guys I work with has the flu and I'm covering. Maybe after that I'll celebrate, see if my friends want to grab a drink with me.

MisterHaven: Do I need to remind you to be careful? Designated driver, park in a well-lit location, no taking drinks from guys you don't know, all that good stuff?

LanieLove: Lol. Nope. I AM a mature adult, so I don't NEED you to remind me...

LanieLove: But I love and appreciate that you do.

And then she sent him one of those little smiley-faces with a red-heart-kiss.

He shook his head as he put the phone back in his pocket and called up his payroll spreadsheet on the computer. Oh, how the mighty had fallen. Master Blake—tied in knots by a stubborn, insolent female he knew all too well, and melted into goo by a female he barely knew at all.

A FEW HOURS LATER, a soft rap on his office door had him glancing up from his computer screen and what he saw had him doing a double-take. It was Slay, cradling a tiny baby on his enormous shoulder.

"Hey, Daff said you wanted to see me?" Slay whispered, stepping into the room.

Slay was the tallest and broadest of all the guys who worked at The Club. With his shaved head, numerous tattoos, and scruffy beard, he was almost certainly the most *feared* of all the guys. Which was why Blake had a hard time reconciling himself to the vision that appeared before him.

"Uh, yeah," Blake whispered back, then shook his head at his own foolishness, and continued in a slightly louder voice. "Yeah, take a seat if you want." He gestured to the chair where Daphne had sat earlier.

"Nah, I'm good," Slay said. He took a step closer, but remained standing, his six-and-a-half-foot bulk towering over Blake, the desk, and everything else in the room.

And then the baby cradled against Slay's shoulder made a noise —not a cry, more like a whimper or a sigh, and Slay began to rock, his entire enormous bulk swaying from side to side, one muscled forearm braced under the infant's diaper-clad butt while his other broad hand moved in wide circles around the infant's back, soothing her. The baby nestled her head further into the crook of Slay's neck, and settled back to sleep.

"Holy shit, you're good at that," Blake commented.

Slay shrugged. "It's a gift."

Blake smirked. "Matteo know you ran off with his daughter?"

Slay smiled broadly. "Oh, yeah. Frankie started fussing loud enough to scream his ear off, so he let me take her."

"And she settled down for you." It was a statement not a question, but Slay answered it anyway.

"Yup. She always does. Drives Matt ballistic, but what can I say?" Slay's grin was infectious. "I'm kind of a baby whisperer."

Blake snorted. "I bet it drives him ballistic. Just like it drives Hillie ballistic when you call Francesca 'Frankie.'"

Slay chuckled. "Pretty much. But you know, you love your kid, you give her what's best for her, even if that means handing her off to Uncle Alex. Isn't that right, *Frankie?*" he cooed. "Driving your daddy bat-poop crazy was just a side benefit."

The baby didn't reply, but Blake couldn't help himself.

"Bat-poop?"

Slay leveled a glance at him. "You heard me. Gotta clean up the language," he declared.

Blake blinked, then smiled. "You do know she can't understand you yet, right?"

"Yep. But Charlie does," Slay countered, rolling his eyes. "Kid understands, *and repeats*, every damn-er, *dar*n—thing I say. Allie says he's gonna have the most colorful vocabulary in third grade if I don't watch myself."

Blake nodded and let the warmth of the scene envelop him for half a second. Slay, his right-hand man and trusted friend, holding their other friend's baby, while talking about the boy Slay was making plans to formally adopt. Blake had had no idea when he'd started this place, this club for people who enjoyed kink like he did, that The Club would be a catalyst for building these bonds, these *families*. The idea moved him profoundly, and made him more determined than ever to protect them.

"You talked to Matt about our new email pen pal?" Blake asked, getting to the point of the meeting. He grabbed the payroll sheet off the printer, and a pen from the glass jar Daff kept stocked on his desk.

Slay's lips twitched. "The Church of the Highest Prophet? Yeah, he mentioned it. Sounds like someone trying to get some publicity at our expense."

Blake nodded and tapped the pen against the desk. "He told you about the pictures?"

Slay lifted his chin. "Better than that, I've looked at them myself. One of the front awning, and one of *your* handsome mug," he said grimly. "What's your take on it?"

"I'm not sure," Blake said, leaning back in his chair, eyes to the ceiling as he toyed with the pen. "I'm inclined to agree with your assessment. Some pop-up preacher is trying to increase his fame—and the donations to his church—by attacking the friendly neighborhood BDSM club he figures everyone loves to hate. But I can't quite reconcile myself to it. Something about it feels... off. Personal. I can't put my finger on it." He lowered his eyes to find Slay watching him. "We shouldn't take any chances."

"Take chances," Slay repeated. "What are you talking about?"

"This church seems to want its members to rile their local politicians and their neighbors to take action against us. What if they aren't just making mischief, but trying to *discredit* us, shut us down, even?"

Slay snorted. "Like you'd ever shut this place down just because some pansy-ass took a picture of you. You're not ashamed of the way you live your life. That email is just free publicity for The Club!"

Blake snorted. "No shit," he confirmed. "But it won't take long for the Prophet to realize that. He's already escalated from blanket hate mail to something far more personal. What's the next step in the game, Slay? Hell, what's the *end*game?"

Slay watched him closely for a moment, but when he said nothing, Blake continued.

"This guy is going to realize he can't do a damn thing by taking pictures of *me* or *you* or *Matt*. Hell, they could post a picture of *you* with a caption that says '*Satan!*' and you'd frame the damn thing."

Slay snorted.

"But what if they took a picture of *Allie* coming into work and captioned it with the words 'Satan's Bride!' or some shit? What if they see Dom come in, and one of the followers is a potential client?" He paused for a moment before dropping the biggest bomb. "What about *Elena?*"

Slay looked at him speculatively for a moment, as though seeing more behind Blake's words than Blake had intended. Then Slay lifted his chin.

"What are you suggesting?" he asked, his voice subdued.

"I'm suggesting... caution. That's all. For the time being, maybe you and the guys wanna hang with your women at *Cara*, instead of here. I'm thinking we institute a new rule that employees and their families *must* park in the employee lot. For the time being, no access to The Club for non-members, including guests. If these assholes are trying to land a punch on us, we wanna minimize the number of available targets."

Slay nodded. "What's your timeframe?"

"As long as it takes to make sure this group is harmless, and that their threats are no more than scare tactics," Blake told him, glancing down to scrawl his signature at the bottom of the payroll sheet. "Which means, as long as it takes you and your team to dig into these guys. And if we find out they're after something more than an easy scapegoat to gain publicity, we'll have to make sure the Prophet, uh, *sees the light*."

Slay's face contorted in a grimace. "Jesus. That was awful."

Blake stood and grinned, before turning around to a tall file cabinet against the wall and opening the drawer. "That was *excellent*. You're just pissed you didn't think of it."

Slay shook his head, but his mouth twitched. "This is what you do at night, huh? Lie awake, thinking of shitty puns?"

Blake froze, his entire body solid as Slay's joking taunt penetrated. What would Slay do if he knew just what Blake *really* did when he was lying awake at night? It would be an end to their easy friendship, that was for damn sure.

Blake made himself move, finding the correct folder and filing the paper in his hand, forced his voice to be light as he turned to Slay and smirked.

"That what *you* do at night? Lie there wondering what *I'm* doing? Slay, I'm touched, really. I just wouldn't want Allie to get the wrong idea, you know?"

Slay's eyes lit with humor, and his chuckle was a rumble too low to wake the baby. "Peace," he said, holding out a placating hand. "I shoulda known better than to start shit with you, man."

Blake snorted. *Damn straight.*

"All right, call me if you need me," Slay said. "I'm out of here for the night. Matt's probably ready to have me arrested for kidnapping, and Allie's gonna send out a search party. More than one babygirl needs her Daddy."

Blake chuckled and held out a hand, which Slay shook firmly.

"Drive safely and tell Allie I say hi," Blake said as he resumed his seat.

He looked up a moment later to find Slay staring at him with uncharacteristic hesitation.

"What's up?" Blake asked.

"About the other night," Slay said, "when we were all hanging here at The Club."

The night he'd had words with Elena by her car. The night the picture of him had been taken. "What about it?"

"You and Elena got into it. She goaded you. She was out of line. It's been eating at me for days, and I wanted to apologize—"

Blake held up a hand and scowled. "Jesus, Slater! I don't want an apology from you. She and I are both adults, and we happen to push each other's buttons."

Slay nodded. "Yeah, I know you're right. I think I got in the habit a long time ago of thinking of her like my kid, you know?" He lifted his hand from Frankie's back to smooth it over his head, then winced. "She'd kill me if she knew I'd said that."

"Yeah, she would." And Blake wouldn't entirely blame her.

Slay grimaced.

"Though, considering you're still breathing after what you said the other night right in front of her..." Blake goaded.

"What'd I say?" Slay demanded.

"I threatened to spank her, and you volunteered to hold her down!" Blake reminded him.

"Oh, shi... I mean, *shoot!* Yeah. But that's only because I knew you wouldn't," Slay told him. "When it comes down to it, I trust you with her, you know? You're pretty much the only single guy in Boston I can say that about."

Blake nodded, even as he felt his stomach twist with guilt. "That… means a lot," he choked out.

But as Slay and Frankie departed, Blake wondered whether guilt would be enough to banish Elena from his dreams.

CHAPTER 4

*E*lena stretched her arms up over her head, yawning like a kitten just waking from slumber, realizing she felt more well-rested than usual. She listened for a moment as the birds tweeted out her window, enjoying the pleasurable sounds of early spring, before she bolted upright. What time was it? Holy crap, the light out the window was *way* too bright to be five a.m. She grabbed frantically at her phone on the bedside table, and hit the power button. Her jaw dropped when she looked at the time. 6:45! It wasn't until she was flying out of her bed, blankets askew around her, that she realized she had four messages on her phone from MisterHaven.

MisterHaven: Good morning, sunshine.

Sent at 5:30, the time she was supposed to have gotten up. Then, fifteen minutes later:

MisterHaven: Lanie? You awake yet?

And fifteen minutes after that:

MisterHaven: I'm afraid you may have slept through your alarm. Rise and shine, kiddo!

The latest was sent just three minutes ago.

MisterHaven: Please message me as soon as you get this so I know you're okay.

Groaning out loud, trying to text with one hand while hopping around trying to pull on her scrubs with her other hand, she texted back. *Awake. Overslept. Later.*

She ran to her bathroom, splashed cold water on her face, and slapped toothpaste on a toothbrush while glancing at herself in the mirror. She froze, toothbrush half paused mid-brush. She looked like *shit.* Her long black hair was straggly and unkempt, bluish circles underscored her eyes, emphasized with smudged mascara from her late night over at Dom and Heidi's the night before. She'd finally made it to their place for dinner, but had stayed far longer than she should have. The phone on the vanity buzzed obnoxiously as she finished brushing her teeth, ran a brush through her hair, and grabbed at her makeup case. With a sigh, she dabbed on cover-up to hide the dark circles, ran a mascara brush through her lashes, and slid lip gloss across her lips. She shrugged. Marginally better.

Picking up her phone, she saw she had a reply from MisterHaven, but she waited to open it. She'd have a few minutes to catch her breath on the train into work, and she could message him then. With a groan, she shot a text to her charge nurse. *Running late. Be there in thirty.* She'd be a full half-hour late to start, if she was lucky.

Her reply came back seconds later. *I need you ASAP. We have thirty-two week twins, three women in active labor, and two nurses in the OR for a stat C-section.*

Elena groaned and yelled out loud to her phone. "Sure, let me just summon my private jet. Dumbass!" She shoved her phone in her bag, raced to the kitchen, grabbed a banana and one of the chocolate protein bars MisterHaven had recommended she grab "in case of emergencies," and looked longingly at her coffee pot. No time. She'd have to grab a cup of swill at the train station.

Ten minutes later, she was running along Main Street, her hair flying behind her, as she had a train to catch.

"Wait!" she shouted, waving her arm frantically as she could see the outbound train she needed, just on the other side of the entry gate. Her fingers flew through her bag, grabbed her CharlieCard, the monthly pass for the Boston subway system known to locals simply as "the T," and shoved it into the slot to let her pass through the gates.

"Easy, girl, you're not gonna get anywhere faster by knocking someone over," said the conductor, but Elena didn't even look at him as the doors to the gate opened and she raced through to the platform. Too late. As she watched, the silver doors slid shut, and she was left bereft as the last outbound train for fifteen minutes pulled away. Her card still held in one hand, her protein bar and banana in the other, her shoulders slumped, defeated. She closed her eyes briefly, ignoring the stares from the others around her still waiting for the inbound train, as she went to find a vacant bench.

A lump rose in her throat and she rapidly blinked tears away as she found a small bench in a cool, dank corner. In the distance she heard the low, melancholy tunes of a saxophone. It was not uncommon for musicians to perform somewhere in the corridors or platforms of the downtown subway system. They'd toss a baseball cap or empty guitar box in front of them, and play to their hearts' content, while locals would toss spare change and singles to them. It was a quirky thing she liked about being a local in downtown Boston. It somehow gave character to the well-worn streets. But today, the notes of the sax only seemed to make her want to cry that much more.

She slumped against the bench and pulled out her cell phone, swiping and effectively ignoring the irate messages from her charge nurse, a text from Alex, and a picture of baby Francesca from Hillie. God, was *everyone* in the world up before she was?

The only one she felt like messaging at all was the one at the very top of her screen.

MisterHaven: I'm sorry you overslept. Message me when you have a quiet minute. Thinking of you.

She blinked back the tears even harder as she responded. *I just missed my train. Sitting waiting for the next one that won't come for another FREAKING fifteen minutes, while my manager virtually lambastes me, my head is pounding from lack of coffee, and apparently everyone in the world is awake on time and earlier than me today.*

She put her phone down as she angrily tore the peel off the banana and ate half of it in one large bite. She chewed and swallowed furiously, as if it were her breakfast's fault she was late. Next she tore the cellophane off the protein bar and took a large bite, but as she chewed, she moaned out loud. She'd completely forgotten her water bottle, and she forgot how the bar stuck in her mouth like peanut butter. She wrapped the rest of the bar up and stuck it in her pocket, popped the rest of the banana in her mouth, and tossed the peel in a nearby garbage basket.

Her phone buzzed, and she picked it up hopefully.

MisterHaven: That sucks, sweetheart.

Her lip stuck out and she pouted, nodding to the phone, thinking, *"Yes, sir, it does. It really really does!"*

Another message popped up.

MisterHaven: Why did you oversleep?

Guilt niggled at her conscience. She swallowed, again wishing she had that bottle of water, as she responded.

LanieLove: I was out late with friends, and had a few drinks. Looks like I set my alarm for p.m. instead of a.m. I do that sometimes like a total spaceshot.

MisterHaven: Don't call yourself names, Lanie. You're not a spaceshot. You had a lot on your mind this week. Tonight, I'll remind you to set your alarm properly. I think it's best you plan on getting to bed a little on the early side. Can you do that, honey?

She swallowed. Why did he care? And why did it feel so nice that he did? Could she possibly be falling for a man she'd never even met?

LanieLove: Thanks, MisterH. I'd like that.

MisterHaven: Now let's talk about how we're going to prevent this from happening again.

The sternness in his tone set her heart to pounding. She bit her lip, and couldn't help but egg him on a little.

LanieLove: Uh oh. Am I in trouble?

God, why was it suddenly thrilling to be on the receiving end of a lecture from him? Weren't people supposed to dislike getting scolded? Yet, her heart pitter-pattered in her chest waiting for his reply.

MisterHaven: If you were mine? Absolutely.

The tempo of her heartbeat accelerated. She took a deep breath before she replied. She was playing with fire and she knew it, but she couldn't help herself.

LanieLove: What would you do if I were yours, MisterH?

MisterHaven: It depends, Lanie. I'd likely give you a bedtime. I'd make sure you were getting enough rest. But if you continued to be late, there would be consequences. You read LadyHaven's blog, sweetheart. What do YOU think I'd do?

Oh, *God.* She almost dropped her phone. She closed her eyes briefly, arousal pooling in her belly, before she responded.

LanieLove: I seem to recall you having a certain fondness for um, spanking.

MisterHaven: Bingo. This kinda behavior would find you bent over my knee. But I'd try to help you figure out what the root of your tardiness was. What do you think would help you get to bed on time?

The screeching of the approaching train snapped her out of her conversation. God, all she needed was to somehow miss *this* one and be even later to work. She shoved her phone in her bag and jumped to her feet, as the train pulled up and the doors swung open. It was positively teeming with people, but she managed to push past everyone and find a place where she could stand and hold onto the loop hanging from the metal bars, to brace herself when the train accelerated. When the train began to go, she opened up her phone again and typed one-handed.

Damn. He expected an answer.

LanieLove: You're right. A good spanking would help a LOT of things right about now.

She looked out the window, suddenly wistful, as the pine trees and maples sped past in a blur of green. Her phone didn't buzz for a moment, and when it did, she took a deep breath before she looked at the screen.

Her cheeks flamed, and she closed her eyes as arousal pulsed within her just *reading* his response. She'd never even seen a picture of him, but somehow conjured up an imagine of a large, stern man with large hands, and piercing blue eyes, who looked remarkably like… nope. She wasn't gonna go there.

MisterHaven: Agreed.

She sent one final text before she shoved her phone in her bag.

LanieLove: I am at work now. I'll message later. My shift is over at seven. Sound good? You have a good day.

MisterHaven: Sounds great. You, too, honey. Xox

She smiled to herself as she exited the train, but when she stepped out, ready to trot the quarter mile to the hospital, her expression fell. A few well-dressed men and women walked past her with signs. She froze mid-stride as the black and white photograph plastered on the side of the poster board they were carrying caught her attention. She knew that place on the board so well it was like her second home: The Club. Wide-eyed, mouth agape, Elena craned her neck, but could only read a few words. *Lechery! Abuse!*

She gasped. What the actual *fuck* was that all about?

But there was no time to ponder, or even worry, as her phone buzzed *again.* Her boss.

Where ARE you?????

Groaning out loud, she hit the power button on the side of the phone, zipped it in her bag, and began to jog her way to the hospital.

ELENA SAT upright in her chair at the clinic, the only chair she'd comfortably sat in all day long. She'd been volunteering here for several years, and though it was tiring to volunteer after a full day at the hospital, it was always nice to go from the intensity of the labor and delivery floor, where she hardly had time to pee let alone sit, to the calmer, more peaceful atmosphere of *Centered*. Unlike the other more medically-oriented women's clinics in downtown Boston, *Centered* was a non-profit whose goal was to help women find a peaceful sanctuary. They could find a nurse or counselor to talk to them, seek assistance if they were in an abusive situation, or find the medical supplies they sometimes needed. *Centered* encouraged positivity and wellness, and was a place where self-care was promoted. Elena loved it. It was easier putting in the long hours knowing she was helping others who could really benefit from talking to a trained nurse.

Yesterday, she'd helped a young woman hear the heartbeat of her baby for the very first time, listened to another mother who needed a shoulder to cry on after suffering a miscarriage, and celebrated the engagement of a volunteer who'd gotten a proposal at the Red Sox game the night before. Though her days were busy and her schedule full, she liked knowing how she spent her time had purpose and worth. But now, she straightened in her chair as two women sat in front of her with tear-stained cheeks.

"Tell me again what you just said," Elena asked calmly, folding her hands on her lap. *Centered* was considered a "safe haven," a place where women could go to report abuse without fear of judgment.

One woman, a thin blonde with high cheekbones and a pointed nose, wiped a tissue across her eyes. Elena watched her warily, as her eyes went to her friend's. The woman's friend sat across from her, wearing a skin-tight pink halter top and equally tight black skirt. Her curly brown hair was pulled back in a messy ponytail, and she was snapping gum as she patted her friend's knee. Though *Centered* saw women from all walks of life, there was something not *quite* right about these two, though she couldn't put her finger on it. She didn't trust them.

"We decided we wanted to go have a little fun," she said, "try out a few things we really hadn't yet. And we heard that the best place to get some kinky action in Boston was The Club."

Elena froze, her breath catching in her throat as she feigned ignorance. "Oh?" she said, encouraging the girl to continue.

"Yes," the blonde nodded, her eyes widening. "After BlackBox closed down, there weren't a lot of places to go, and we heard The Club was classy. So, we went."

She'd make a note to ask Alex if he'd seen the two, though he saw so many women come in and out of The Club on a daily basis, that it was unlikely he'd be helpful.

Elena nodded, as the blonde continued. "And when we got there, it was fun. We met a few guys, and one dom who said he'd introduce us to some other people. We had a few drinks…" she shrugged, her voice trailing off as she looked at her friend.

The brunette picked up where her friend left off. "Yep. We both had a few drinks. And they must've been drugged by the dom or something, because the next thing you know, we found ourselves in a back room, and we were both *stripped* and *bruised* and tied up!"

Elena blinked. No way. This could not be happening. "You think someone drugged you and took advantage of you?" she asked.

The blonde nodded vigorously. "We don't *think* it. We know it." She sniffed. "The Club is all about 'safe, sane, consensual,' but drugging women and taking advantage of them isn't any of those things!" She frowned. "We thought we were safe there."

Elena frowned. "Did you go to the police?"

The brunette shook her head. "No. We don't trust the police. But Denise's boyfriend hit her last year, and you guys helped her find a lawyer and stuff, without going to the police. So, we came here first. We know our rights."

Elena sighed. "When did this happen?" she asked.

"Last night," the brunette said, casting her eyes down. Damn.

Though they seemed untrustworthy, Elena had to investigate further. Under ordinary circumstances, she'd try to get the women to go to the police, but that didn't seem to be the best strategy at this juncture.

Elena nodded. "I'm so sorry," she said. "How did you two manage to get out?"

They looked at each other for a moment before the blonde started talking rapidly. "My restraints were loose!" She said. "I managed to get out and then untied both of us. We grabbed our clothes and got the hell out of there."

Elena blinked, then nodded again. "I'm sorry, girls. Why don't I put you with one of our counselors who can help you with this? Okay?"

She stood, and the two tear-stained women followed her. Elena introduced them to Nadia, the volunteer counselor, who ushered the women into her office.

Nadia, a middle-aged Russian woman with thick brown hair looped into a wide braid, smiled at her. Nadia and Elena had been friends for years, and worked together at *Centered* for even longer. Nadia had been married for twenty years, had three adult children, and volunteered regularly at the clinic. Though she'd lived on American soil for the entirety of her marriage, she still had a slight Russian accent. "Going for a stroll, honey?" she asked, her words meticulously pronounced.

Elena hadn't been planning on leaving quite yet, but the idea of a walk sounded perfect. She nodded. "Text me if you need me," she said, leaning in to whisper. "Not so sure I trust these two."

Nadia nodded, her smile unwavering. She'd been around the block a time or two, and knew how to handle the situation. "Got it. Let's chat later, okay?"

"Absolutely," Elena called over her shoulder as she took her leave.

It felt good to be outside for a bit. She felt unsettled by what the girls had told her, and the more she thought about it, the more fired-up she got. Their story couldn't possibly true… could it? The clinic was just a few blocks away from Queensborough Street, where The Club was located. She was going to take a walk, all right, and she knew exactly where she was going. She was curious how Blake would respond to such blatant accusations. Her phone buzzed, and she glanced at the screen.

Alex: Hey. I'm not heading into The Club tonight, and I don't want you going there until we've talked.

Furrowing her brow, she wondered what that was about, at the same moment another text came in, reminding her that MisterHaven had asked her to check in with him an hour ago. Damn!

MisterHaven: Hey. I thought you were gonna text me an hour ago. Lanie? You okay?

She groaned out loud as she responded.

LanieLove: Um, yeah. I'm sorry, got totally distracted and forgot to text. I'm doing okay. You?

Between the conversation she'd just had at *Centered,* followed by the text from Alex, and now from MisterHaven, she was starting to get pretty pissed off.

MisterHaven's response didn't come for a moment, but when it did, she bit her lip.

MisterHaven: I'm good. But you're pushing it, little girl.

What did *that* mean?

She frowned.

LanieLove: Yeah? What is that supposed to mean?

There was no response for a minute, as her anger got the better of her. Having started off the day on the wrong foot, the crazy busy day at work delivering not one but *two* sets of multiples, then heading to *Centered* only to have the women say that her *very favorite place in the world* was responsible for women being victimized? Now MisterHaven, the one and only *man* she really trusted beside her *brother,* was gonna go all dom on her because she forgot to text him? What was this, some type of twisted reality show?

Her phone buzzed and for a minute she glared at it, before she realized she was shooting negative energy at the one friend who'd had her back more than anyone. What the hell had come over her?

MisterHaven: Yes. Lanie, you need to settle down. I'm just worried about you, and trying to help, and it seems you're giving me attitude at every juncture. And frankly? I don't like that.

She sighed. But she'd come to the entrance to the large, nondescript brownstone at 826 Queensborough. Squaring her shoulders, she faced the entrance, opened the door, and nodded curtly to the two bouncers whose warm smiles dissolved when they took in her pissed-off expression. They stepped back. No one messed with Alex Slater; therefore, no one messed with Alex Slater's kid sister. Elena knew this well, and today, she was grateful that they all gave her wide berth. She knew Alex wasn't here at the moment, which was unfortunate, because she had shit to discuss, and she wanted to discuss it *now,* which *further* meant that the man she'd have to talk to was Blake, and God if he didn't piss her off.

She picked up her phone and shot off a quick text.

LanieLove: Thanks for the concern. Long, long, day. I'm fine. Will text in a bit.

She marched past the bar, where Alice waved to her before Elena stormed past, noticing that The Club was filling up with members now that it was getting into early evening. Blake's office was at the very back of the main floor, and set up with enough video cameras that if Blake was in the office, he'd see her coming. The large door to his office was slightly ajar which stopped her *not at all* as she shoved the palm of her hand flat against it, feeling the satisfying *smack* as the door swung open. He was leaning up against his desk, cell phone in hand, and when she walked in, he hit a button that looked like *send* and placed his phone down as if he'd been expecting her. He folded his arms across his chest, his eyes focused on her with an unreadable expression and a smile that didn't quite meet his eyes.

"Elena," he greeted.

She stopped just two feet in front of him. *"Blake,"* she spat back, ignoring the fact that storming in here like this was really pretty rude, and that she could've at least called or taken a breather before she went on a fact-finding mission with Blake as the target of her irritability and angst after a shitty day.

Whatever.

Her phone buzzed in her hand. Given the fact that for one quick minute she actually *wanted* an excuse to take her eyes off the ones that were burning a hole straight through her, she picked up her phone and glanced at the screen.

MisterHaven: No problem, honey.

Just to piss Blake off, she decided to be rude and respond while Blake waited for her.

LanieLove: Thanks. I'll be back in a bit.

As she put her phone in her purse, ready to find out what the *fuck* was going on, and whether or not Alex's admonition not to come to The Club had anything to do with the accusations the women back at *Centered* made, the phone on his desk buzzed. Blake looked at his phone and she stared, as bits and pieces began to connect.

No.

Widower. Long-term dominant. Busier in the evenings than during the day. No children.

No!

Her eyes met his, and she realized he was connecting the dots at the very moment she had. Her eyes widened, her jaw dropped, and she gaped, as his jaw clenched.

"No *fucking* way," she whispered, her head shaking from side to side.

He glared at the message on his phone, fingers swiping as he replied. Seconds later, her phone predictably buzzed.

"Yes *fucking* way," he said, as he shook his head in wonder, the fury rolling off him confirming that he'd been every bit as ignorant about the truth as she'd been.

All she could do was stare.

He was the first to move. With painfully controlled movements, he stalked to his office door, slammed it, and hit the lock, then turned, marching toward her with a heat she felt down to the tips of her toes. She'd never *seen* him so mad, and for reasons she couldn't quite fathom, she felt her panties dampen as her thighs clenched and she backtracked toward his desk, her hands flailing out behind her, while her mind played over and over, *"No way, no way, no way, no way."*

He stalked toward her until her ass hit his desk, and she had no choice but to bend backward to avoid colliding with him. He towered over her, placed both hands on the desk on either side of her, his blue eyes glaring. His brows were drawn together, nostrils flared, and the power that emanated from him had her heart pounding in ways she couldn't decipher. Now that he was close, she could smell the woodsy scent of raw masculinity and anger, and he pressed up against her, the heat of his body overtaking her as the length of his rock-hard erection confirmed she wasn't the only one who was *fucking turned on.*

"I've got nowhere else to go," she whispered. "And you're scaring me."

It was scary in a *good* way, the way she felt when one of the doms tied her wrists or unfastened the buckle of his belt, fear dancing with arousal, the knowledge deep down in her bones that this wasn't *safe*, this wasn't *gentle*, but fuck if she didn't want to taste every last bit of the delicious power he wielded.

"Scaring you?" he whispered in her ear, one hand bracing himself on the desk as another threaded fingers through her hair, looping the midnight black locks around his enormous fingers and tugging her head back. She couldn't help it, as the moan came from deep within her. She was panting, could feel the rise and fall of her chest as she gasped for air. She was drowning, and he was pushing her in even deeper. "I'm *scaring* you?" he rasped. "Little girl, I haven't even begun."

He held her head back, the pull along her scalp tingling in delicious pain, as he continued to whisper. "You knew, didn't you, *Lanie?* You knew it was me, and you played me like a fucking instrument."

The accusation hit her straight in the solar plexus, and she lost the last thread of self-control holding her together.

"Fuck *you!*" she fumed, her hands hitting his chest so hard she could feel the slap in her palms, trying fruitlessly to push him off of her, and he didn't budge an inch. "I didn't fucking *know! God!* You think I knew? You think I'd pour my heart out to *you?* You think I…"

But she got no further as he stepped back, nabbed both of her wrists, pinned them down to her side and spun her around. With a sweep of his massive hand across his desk, papers and pens and paperclips went flying, bouncing off the floor and the chair. He placed both of her hands on the desk, and pushed her torso so that she was flush against the gleaming cherry wood surface. She struggled against him but was completely overpowered. Holding his hand against the small of her back, his other rose and fell, a searing smack landing straight across her ass. She howled and twisted, but couldn't get away, one blistering spank after another landing. Her ass was on fire as her whole body teemed with arousal.

A dim part of her brain wanted to tell him to stop, but she couldn't, because even in the moment she knew this was *exactly* what she needed. After half a dozen hard swats, he turned her around to face him, one huge hand engulfing her chin and bringing her eyes to his. "You don't swear at me," he growled. "You don't tell me what to do." His blue eyes pierced hers. "From now on, we lay our cards on the table and you'll fucking be honest with me. Yeah?"

She gasped and could only nod her head, as a split second later, his mouth was on hers and *fucking hell,* it was the best kiss she'd ever had in her life. His lips met hers hard, the possessive feel of them as powerful and fierce as he was. She moaned as his tongue touched hers. He'd broken the seal, and now a floodgate of emotion raced through her veins.

Pushed up against the desk, her ass burned from the spanking he'd given her. As he continued to ravage her, his fingers raked her blouse up. As his rough, hard hand found her breast, her knees buckled. God, the man fucking knew how to touch a woman. Her nipples were hard, her body limp at his mercy, her clit zinged with arousal and her core pulsed with the need to feel him.

This wasn't just the arrogant asshole she'd been crushing on for months. This wasn't just the severe, distant owner of The Club. This was the man who'd helped her get her shit together when no one else could. This was the man who'd listened to her pour her heart out, watching over for her with an almost paternal gentleness —steady, stern, and unyielding.

He pulled his mouth off hers just long enough to whisper a heated, furious, desperate, *"Elena."*

Her voice unnaturally low, pled with him. "God, I'm sorry I've been such a bitch."

His forehead up against hers, he grinned, actually *grinned*, those wrinkles around his eyes creasing. "You'll pay for those bitchy comments, little girl," he crooned in her ear. Her eyes closed as heat flared across her chest.

"Make me pay," she begged. "Make me *fucking pay.*"

She heard the sound of his belt buckle unfastening. *God.* Was he going to fuck her or spank her, and did it *even matter?* She wanted all of it. She wanted all of *him.* The swish of the leather being pulled through the loops made her legs clench. She opened her eyes and bit her lip as he took his belt in hand, doubled it over, spun her around, and pushed her back up against the desk.

"You wanna pay?" he growled in her ear.

"*Yesss,*" she moaned. The buckle hit the desk seconds before his hands reached to the front of her scrubs, nimbly pulling the drawstring and shoving them down, along with her panties, so she could step out. He took one moment to draw his hand across her inner thigh before he pushed her legs apart, positioning them so her ass was on prominent display. God, she was bared to Blake and she'd never been so turned on in her life. *Fuck*, could he see her honey glistening on her thighs? She was gonna come just from being stripped by him.

The cool of the desktop hit her cheek as he firmly positioned her, head down, ass bared. She heard him pick up the belt again, and she wanted it, she *needed* to be marked by him. The whiz and *snap* of his belt made her shriek as he lashed her, pain and heat suffusing together, but it wasn't unbearable. It was delicious, and she arched her back for more. Another swing, and heat striped her ass.

"You'll do as you're told," he growled, before the smack of leather hit her naked skin again.

She could only nod, wanting more, wanting *harder*, and somehow he knew, as he reared back and snapped his belt against her again, and again, and *again*. Her ass was on fire, her clit throbbed with need, her eyes shut tight as she took the spanking she'd been craving like a drowning woman craved air. She heard the belt hit the floor, and the telltale sounds of his own jeans being unfastened.

Yes.

With his hands on either side of her hips, he pulled her to him, his erection pressed up against her, warm, and hard as flint. His mouth came to her ear. "You gonna be a good girl?" he growled.

She grinned, spreading her legs for him. "Fuck *no*," she said, earning a wicked tug of the hair just seconds before he thrust his cock between her legs. She was so ready for him, slick and heated, and it felt so fucking good being filled by him.

Arousal ripped through her, tearing her apart in the most delicious way possible with every thrust of his hips. Flames leapt across her chest and her clit pounded. She wanted him, *needed* him, her pussy milking his cock for what he had to give her. He pulled her hair, making her scream as a savage thrust had her about toppling over the edge.

"Brat," he growled.

"Mmmm," was her only response. He smacked her thigh hard with the flat of his hand, and the touch sent her over the edge. She screamed, her head thrown back as she climaxed. Fuck, she'd never come like this, the orgasm tearing through her body with abandon, electric shocks of pleasure zinging through every inch of her, and as she came, hard and long, she heard him grunt his own release.

"Fuck, baby," he growled, moaning into her hair as they both gave way to ecstasy. The thrusts slowed with every beat of her heart, until she lay, limp and sated, across the cool top of his desk.

"Oh my God," she whispered. He said nothing, but leaned down and kissed her cheek, the prickle of his whiskers a delicious contrast to the warm, tender feel of his lips.

"Easy, baby," he said. "Stay right there. I'm gonna take care of you now, honey." Who was this man? Blake had never spoken to her with such gentleness, but this wasn't just Blake, this was *MisterHaven.*

He pulled out. She moaned at the loss of him, but another kiss on her cheek comforted her.

As her heartbeat slowed, her eyes still shut tight with her face pressed up against his desk, her mind finally began to waken.

What the *hell* had they just done?

CHAPTER 5

"What the hell. Daphne?" Blake called through the open office door. And then a split second later, repeated more loudly, "*Daphne!*"

Daphne stuck her head in his door and regarded him with wide eyes. "Y-yes, Boss?"

"What the fuck is this shit?" he demanded, brandishing a paper at her, before turning his attention to the stack of checks on his desk awaiting signatures and scratching out his name.

Daphne took a cautious shuffle-step forward and leaned over to glance at the paper, while one slim finger grabbed a lock of her long, red-gold hair and began to twist it. "I-it's an invoice?" she suggested.

Blake threw the pen in his hand down on the desk and huffed out a breath, feeling a flare of annoyance in his gut that he *knew* was completely out of proportion to the situation.

"Already fucking know it's an invoice, Daff. My first clue was the word INVOICE in huge block letters at the top of the page. My second clue was that you placed it in the folder on my desk labeled Invoices. My question is, what's the invoice *for*? It's from some landscaping company. In case you haven't noticed," he said acidly, waving a hand in the air to illustrate the building, the street, the neighborhood, the *city* around them. "We don't have *land* to *land*scape."

Daphne took the paper and quickly scanned the rest of the sheet, while her pale forehead creased in concentration.

"Honest to God," Blake grumbled. "I leave you guys in charge for a few months, I think things are fine, and I come back to find bullshit invoices I know nothing about, a fucking church that wants to shut us down that I still don't know *jack* about, and God only knows what…"

"It's from January," Daphne interrupted, her voice low and toneless. "This is the company that came to plow the parking lots and shovel the sidewalks. You authorized it."

Blake closed his eyes. Oh. *Fuck.* Yes, he had.

"And I was about to buzz you to say that Matt and Slay are on their way in. They've got some information on the Church of the Highest Prophet to share with you," Daphne continued in the same flat voice that barely masked her hurt.

Blake sighed. His annoyance evaporated and something colder settled in his gut instead. *Remorse.* He knew exactly what had wound him up today, and it definitely hadn't been Daphne or this random invoice. No, it had been the woman who, with one blistering look, had burned all his doubts about his age, his friendship with Slay, and his own readiness for a committed relationship, into nothing but ash.

The same woman who had flown out of his office two nights ago, and hadn't returned a single *fucking* one of his phone calls or texts since then.

He scrubbed a hand over his face.

"I'm sorry, Daff," he told her, meeting her gray eyes squarely. "I'm having a bad day."

"You were having a bad day yesterday, too," Daphne reminded him. "You yelled at the bouncers about keeping the loading area clear and scared the shit out of Donnie."

Blake stifled a snort. Donnie, all six feet and however many inches of muscled bulk of him, had grown up on the rough streets of South Boston, and had cut his teeth working for his older brother, a bookie who used to work out of a bar down on L Street back in the day. Blake was pretty sure he'd have to do more than yell to scare the shit out of Donnie, but he didn't argue.

"It's been a shitty *week*, then," he told her instead. "I let myself get distracted."

By a tiny scrap of a woman with eyes like coffee and skin like smooth, creamy silk.

Daphne's stormy, gray eyes immediately softened and her mouth twisted into a sympathetic grimace as she stepped closer and set the invoice on his desk. "Ah, geez, of course. *God*. I forget sometimes, you know? Is there anything I can do to help?"

Blake stared at her in confusion for several seconds before light dawned. *Jesus.* She thought he was upset because he was *grieving*. Upset about *Josie*.

And now a new kind of guilt came over him. His evening went from bad to worse.

"Nah, it's not… it's not *that* kind of bad day," honesty compelled Blake to admit. "It was hard losing Josie, and I'm sure I'll continue to have tough days every now and then, but that's not what's bothering me."

"Oh. Well, what is it then?" Her eyes were calm and soothing, her tone so full of friendly sympathy that he didn't have the heart to tell her to back off. "I'm kind of the unofficial therapist in my family, you know? Side benefit to being the youngest. Both of my sisters vent to me all the time about their asshole men and their crazy kids. My mom does it too."

Daphne, den mother to the world. Blake could see that.

"And, what? You tell them what to do?" Blake asked, leaning back in his chair while one side of his mouth quirked up in a smile he couldn't suppress.

"Not quite." Daphne snickered. "Giving orders is more *your* M.O. than mine, as you know."

Blake laughed and conceded this point. Daphne was one of the strongest women he knew—she'd endured much in her life, and she didn't take shit from Blake or anyone else, but she was by nature a submissive.

"So, what's up?" Daff prompted, when Blake remained silent, lost in his thoughts.

"Huh?"

"Do you want to talk?" she clarified. "About anything? I just listen. And I don't judge."

"Thank you, honey," he told her gently. "But I'm good for now."

"Okay," she agreed. "Just remember that I'm here if you need me." She stood up to leave. "I'll let you know when Slay and Matt get here."

Blake nodded despite the fact that he had a security feed on his computer, and would likely know they were here before Daphne did. He was touched by her offer of friendship. "Thanks again."

Daphne nodded and turned for the door, her red-blonde hair swinging like a sleek curtain down to her hips as she walked, though Blake hardly noticed. His attention had turned, as it always fucking did, back to Elena.

He grabbed his phone from his pocket. Ten messages, he'd sent. Ten messages in two days, and she hadn't replied once. He'd called her twice, but she hadn't answered. He'd even logged on and messaged her as MisterHaven, wondering if she'd be more likely to talk online, but she hadn't. Things couldn't go on like this. His patience, never his finest quality to begin with, was wearing fucking thin.

Blake tossed his phone on the desk and turned to his computer, clicking over to the security feed and forcing himself to focus. Immediately, a dozen boxes flashed on screen, showing the current situation around each of the twelve primary security cameras. At this time of day, The Club was empty but for a few of the wait staff prepping the bar area for tonight's after-work revelers. Outside, the employee parking lot was practically deserted, and only the occasional pedestrian strolled past the front entrance. All quiet and peaceful, just the way he liked it.

Unlike the chaos of the other night.

He'd been sitting in this very spot two evenings ago, watching the feeds, when he'd seen Elena striding up the walkway, looking like she owned the place. He'd been annoyed at first. He'd warned Slay to keep his sister away from The Club for her own protection, but Elena either hadn't gotten the message or hadn't cared.

Annoyance had faded quickly to amusement, though. Amusement heavily tinged with *arousal*, because *Christ*, that woman was twenty pounds of outrageous sex appeal in a five-pound package, from her lush curves, to the perfect symmetry of her face, to the purposeful way she moved.

It was fucked up, but one of the first things he'd ever noticed about Elena was the way she *walked*. Even months and months ago before he'd ever thought of her in a sexual way, he'd found it fascinating, adorable. Right now, it drove him *crazy*. The woman never walked when she could *stride*—her petite legs ate up the ground with the graceful economy of a woman twice her height, her body nearly hummed with contained energy, and her black hair bounced behind her like the tail of a comet.

Only when she'd entered the main bar area had he seen the set cast of her small chin, the banked fire in her eyes. She'd torn through the packed bar room with single-minded focus, headed in his direction, and his amusement had faded altogether. What had set the firecracker alight this time? Whatever it was, the sight of her had made his heart beat in double time.

The self-confidence that had radiated from her was both a weapon and a shield, deflecting the interest of every guy in the bar like a bulletproof vest, a veritable neon sign screaming *Do Not Approach*. She'd reminded him of a kitten who thought she was a tiger, flipping off the biggest, toughest bouncers in Boston like they were pesky flies, slamming her way through his office door as though she hadn't just entered the inner sanctum of the best-known dominant in Boston.

Christ, what was it about her take-no-prisoners approach to life that made him so insane for her? He was a *dominant*, for God's sake. Given his experience, the reputation he'd built, he was fucking *king* of the dominants. And yet, it was no sweet, meek, natural submissive like his Josie who held him in thrall. It was the woman who challenged him with every breath she took.

Make me pay... Make me fucking pay.

Those were the words she'd yelled at him, *screamed* at him, before he'd taken off his belt and applied it to her ass. Marked her as his. Even now, her words had him fighting a rush of arousal, spreading his palm on the desk, just where Elena's cheek had lain that night.

And that's when realization struck him.

He had been going about this all wrong. He'd been sitting back, waiting for her to reply to his texts like a dumbass teenager. He'd been waiting for her to handle her freak-out, to get a grip on whatever the hell had been riding her since the moment he'd pulled out of her sweet pussy the other night, when he'd told her he'd take care of her and she'd turned to him with hard, distant eyes and whispered, "I can't do this right now," before running out the door.

He'd fully expected her to sort her shit and come to him when she was ready.

In other words, he'd allowed himself to be deflected as easily as those guys at the bar.

He slapped his palm on the desk, pissed off at his own stupidity, as the certainty of it settled in his bones. He knew better than this. Instead, he'd allowed his submissive—and there was not a doubt in his mind that Elena *would be* his submissive—to call the fucking shots.

He'd let himself forget that Elena had said *other* things two nights ago, also. She'd promised to be honest with him. She'd promised to put her *cards on the table.* She'd broken those promises.

Wonder if she's still feeling the sting from my belt, he mused.

He'd have to make sure she did.

But before that, they would fucking talk.

Movement on the security feed caught Blake's eye as a big-ass truck pulled into the employee lot. Slay had arrived.

Blake blew out a deep breath and turned the monitor off.

He wasn't foolish enough to believe that everything would fall into place just because he wanted it to. Slay would clean his clock if he knew what had happened on this desk two nights ago, and Blake wouldn't entirely blame him. He and Slay were friends, even *brothers* of a sort, and he owed the man an explanation and some reassurances. But he also wouldn't allow Slay to dictate how Blake lived his life—or, for that matter, how Elena lived hers.

Life was fucking short. That was the lesson he'd learned through Josie's illness and through seeing his friends struggle to find love and happiness over the past few years. Finding someone who fired him up the way Elena did was a miracle he hadn't even known to look for. He wasn't going to let anything screw that up— not Slay's objections, not Elena's fears, not his own stupidity.

He'd spent the past few months in a daze, letting other people call the shots. But Blake had been reminded in a hundred small ways over the past few weeks that things simply ran more smoothly when *he* took charge.

He wouldn't make that mistake again.

Two seconds after Daphne buzzed to announce his arrival, Slay gave a cursory knock to Blake's open office door and stepped inside.

"Blake, man, what's up?" he greeted with a nod.

Blake stood, extending a hand that Slay took with a powerful grip.

"Not much, brother," Blake said. "You?"

"Allie," Slay said, holding up the phone in his other hand with an expression that was half frustration, half amusement. "She's been sending me cryptic texts for the last fucking hour, asking me when I'm gonna be home and telling me she has plans for tonight."

Blake sat back down and tried to smother a smile. "Ah. And do I wanna ask what her plans are?"

Slay shook his head. "You can ask, but I don't have a clue. Let me tell you, though, what *I've* got planned involves reminding my woman exactly what happens to a little girl who teases her Daddy."

Blake chuckled. "You're a lucky man, Slater."

Slay's eyes shone, and his smile burned bright. "Fucking right, I am," he said softly. Then his eyes sharpened. "Matt here yet?"

Blake shook his head. "You're the first to arrive."

Slay nodded and looked down at his phone again, typing as he spoke. "I think Matt's gotta get Frankie to the sitter before he comes. That's fine. We've got a couple of hours before we have to be anywhere."

"We?" Blake repeated.

"Yeah, me and Elena. She rode in with me and I'm driving her to work tonight—she's got a night shift. She's got something to tell you guys."

Shit. Elena was here? Blake had been dying to talk to her, yes, but he'd imagined their first meeting after the blistering hot sex a few days ago would involve a lot more privacy and a lot *less* Slay. Blake was on a hair trigger, ready to combust from the potent combination of arousal and frustration that Elena always seemed to stir in him, and that would not do with Elena's brother around.

A second later, just as Blake steeled himself to see her, Elena stepped into the room.

She looked pale. That was Blake's first thought. Pale and quiet, as though the life that normally blazed inside her had dimmed since the last time he'd seen her. The dark pink scrubs she wore seemed to dwarf her small frame, she clutched her purse strap as though it were a lifeline, and she crossed the doorway with hesitant steps, as though uncertain whether she was welcome here.

His hands twitched with the need to stand up and grab her, pull her into his lap, and comfort her. He clenched them into fists instead.

Elena hadn't met his eyes, but she caught the way his hands clenched and she swallowed hard. She lifted her face so that her eyes could focus on the wall just over his shoulder.

"Uh, hey," she said, her fingers splaying in a little wave.

"Elena," Blake acknowledged. He'd deliberately made his voice just a little deeper, just a little more commanding than usual, and as he'd expected, her eyes flew to his, responding to the command without her conscious thought.

He watched as emotions swam in her coffee-colored eyes. *Fear. Fatigue. Embarrassment. Relief.* And it was this last one that gave him hope.

He looked at Slay, who was immersed in his phone. "Slater, you mind doing a quick favor for me? Private room three has been rented out for tonight. I asked Donnie and Joe to set it up with all the requested equipment, but I've been up to my eyeballs in paperwork and I haven't had a chance to do the walkthrough. Could you spare a second?"

Slay looked up from his phone and blinked. "Yeah, of course."

"I'd appreciate it," Blake said with a nod. "Daphne has the paperwork. "

Slay stood and headed for the door, requiring Elena to step closer to Blake's desk to let him by. "Hey! Avoid hassling Blake while I'm gone," Slay warned her as he passed. "Try not to jump all over him the second I leave, yeah?"

Elena's pale face flushed nearly purple in an instant, and she sputtered in outrage. "I don't... I wouldn't... What the hell, Alex?"

Slay chuckled to himself as he walked out the door. Blake ran a hand over his mouth to stifle his own laughter. And then her furious eyes found his. And Blake didn't want to laugh anymore.

He was on his feet and heading for the door a second later, and closing it firmly. He hesitated for a single second before deciding *not* to lock it. A locked door would raise too many questions that he didn't want to answer today. Then he whirled to face the woman who'd been haunting him for weeks.

"What do you say, Elena?" he mocked softly. "Feel like jumping all over me?"

Elena's eyes flew to his, and she backed away as he advanced on her, one step, then two, until her ass hit the edge of his desk and she had nowhere to go. She swallowed hard. He took a step closer, boxing her in.

She licked her lips, took a deep breath, and whispered, "I'm sorry."

Blake's head went back and he raised one eyebrow. "Sorry," he repeated thoughtfully, as though testing the weight of the word on his tongue. "*Sorry.* Hmm. That can cover so many things, Elena. I'll need you to be more specific. Sorry you barged into my office the other night spoiling for a fight? Sorry you begged me to take my belt to your luscious ass? Sorry that you *pleaded* for me to own that sweet pussy with my cock? Tell me, honey, what are you sorry for?"

Her eyes had grown wider with each word he spoke, and then impossibly hotter. He could see the pulse pounding in her neck, feel the rapid rise and fall of her breasts against his chest as she panted, but she said nothing. And then he lifted his hand to touch her cheekbone, his fingertip tracing the blush there, and the words seemed to fall out of her.

"None of those things," she whispered. "I'm not sorry I came here. I'm not sorry we had sex. I am definitely not sorry you striped my ass."

She darted a look from his eyes to his mouth, then licked her lips, and Blake fought the urge to grab her, to kiss the life out of her, to use his lips and teeth and tongue to *punish* her for walking out, for leaving him worried and frustrated and pissed off for the last two days. But then she spoke again.

"A-and I'm not sorry I left, either," she told him, her spine straightening, even as his eyes narrowed. "I was overwhelmed, and I just… I couldn't stay."

"You left before we settled a fucking *thing*," he reminded her. "You left while your screams were still echoing in my ears, while I could still taste you on my tongue."

She pushed her lips together, visibly fighting against the effect his words were having on her, but he could see the way her eyes went glassy, the way her body swayed against him.

"And you *stayed* away for two days," he concluded, his voice a low growl as he struggled to control his temper. "Two fucking days, with *no word*. Do you know what that did to me?"

As he watched, her gorgeous brown eyes filled with tears. "That's the part I'm sorry about," she said in a small voice. "I couldn't talk to you the other night. Truly. I was too confused and amped up. I'd had the longest week, and the *worst* day, and I… I just hadn't expected this, *us*, to ever really happen, you know?" She paused and ran a finger under each eye, catching the moisture there. "You have a crush on someone, or in my case, on what you believe to be *multiple* someones," she clarified with a short laugh, "for the longest time, but it's all just a fantasy. There's the smoking hot dom who's the definition of unattainable, the guy I've *wanted* since *forever* ago, but who treats me like a pesky kid sister. And then there's the sweet guy I talk to online, the one who tries to take care of me, but he can never be more than just a fantasy because, God, I don't even know what his hair color is, or where he lives, or when his birthday is, or what kind of kink he's into. And then suddenly, *holy shit*, I'm having sex with you, and it's *both of you*—you *and* MisterHaven, all at once. The guy who revs my engine *and* the guy who's stealing my heart. And I was all worried about doing things wrong, about where we would go from here, about whether I could really *handle* this kind of relationship. It was just… too fast," she whispered.

Blake moved his hand to cradle her neck, his thumb stroking the soft skin beneath her ear, and blew out a breath as he digested this.

Overwhelmed, he could understand. God knew, he'd been dealing with the very same thing. Things *had* happened too fast—tension he now recognized as mutual lust had smoldered between them for months, and then had blazed out of control, like a wildfire.

But he hadn't considered how hard it would be for her to come to grips with the knowledge that he and MisterHaven were one and the same. That process, at least, had been seamless for him—to the point where he'd wondered more than once whether he'd deliberately overlooked all of the evidence that Lanie *was* Elena, since it had allowed him to dominate Elena in the only way he'd thought she'd allow him. But for Elena…

"I could have helped you with that, Lanie," he told her, in a low voice, while his fingers played in her hair. "It's my *job* to help you, to care for you."

"Every time one of your texts came in, I knew, I *knew*, I needed to answer, but I just… didn't know how," she continued, her eyes roving over his face. "The longer things went unresolved, the more I felt like I *couldn't* answer."

Blake closed his eyes briefly and nodded once. *And that part is on you*, he told himself. He shouldn't have let things go so long. He shouldn't have waited.

"Right. Tonight, then, we clear the air," he told her firmly. "Once this business is done, we'll meet up. After your shift, you can come to my place…"

But she shook her head nervously.

"I don't think that's a good idea," she denied.

He raised one eyebrow. "All right, then. I'll go to yours."

She shook her head once more. "I don't think we *should* meet up," she confessed in a whisper. "Not yet."

Blake felt his temper kindle. "Elena, I messed up this week. I should've come to you sooner, should've made you face this head-on. I see that now. If you think I'm going to compound that error by staying away from you now, let you freak out and run away from this…"

She blinked, then frowned in annoyance. "I wasn't *running away*," she said hotly. "I was… Making a strategic retreat. I was contemplating, trying to figure out what I want and what I need."

"Uh huh. And you can figure out if *we*," he lifted his hand from her neck for a moment to gesture between them, "are what you need all by *yourself*? Pretty sure I see a flaw in that logic, baby."

She frowned. "I hadn't thought of it like that."

"How can you possibly know if you want *me*, if you can handle *me*, if I'm gonna give you what you need, if you don't get to know me?" he continued.

"You make a point," she allowed. And then she lifted her hand to his cheek. "But, Blake, just being with you makes thinking *impossible*. You are so physical. So damn *male*. I can't resist you physically. I never could. I'm standing next to you, and my heart is beating a mile a minute. My frickin' nipples are hard, and you're barely touching me. You were looking at me like you wanted to murder me a second ago, and I can feel myself getting… *wet*." Her voice was a husky whisper, and her eyes were alight with… with…

Jesus. His hand tightened against her neck before he forced himself to loosen it.

He wanted so badly to step into her, to put his mouth on her, to overwhelm all her fears and doubts with his own unwavering certainty. In that moment, there was not a doubt in his mind that he could do it. But to what end? That wasn't the certainty that *she* needed, not the kind he wanted her to have. So, instead, he forced himself to take a step back.

"What are you suggesting?" he demanded.

Her eyes got wide, and she smiled—a burst of sunshine that lit up her entire face, the entire damn room. "You *aren't* gonna try to steamroll me, *are* you? I was really worried that you would. Or, more like, I was worried that you wouldn't be able to help yourself, and that I was gonna let you."

He snorted. The day this woman let him steamroll her would be a cold day in hell. "I'm not gonna let you call the shots, LanieLove. Not again. Not ever. But I'll listen to what you have to say. Always."

Her smile grew impossibly brighter. She sucked in a shaky breath and began, "See, MisterHaven, I had this idea…"

Then a burst of laughter out in the entryway startled them both.

BY THE TIME the door opened a few seconds later, Blake was sitting behind his desk, toying with a pen, and Elena was sitting in one of the chairs across from him, her eyes studying her hands which were folded in her lap. Matteo burst into the room, laughing at something Slay had said, and Slay walked in a moment after, carrying a spare chair.

"She behave herself, boss?" Slay asked, earning himself a glare from his sister, and a single raised eyebrow from Blake.

"I think your sister and I have just about come to an understanding," Blake told him. He exchanged a brief glance with Elena, conveying without words that their discussion was most definitely not over and satisfied that she'd gotten the message loud and clear when a pretty blush stole over her face.

As soon as they were all seated and everyone had exchanged greetings, Slay leaned forward in his seat.

"So, Elena share her news with you?" he asked, looking from Blake to Elena.

Elena shook her head. "I was waiting for Matt so I could tell both of them at once," she explained.

Blake frowned. What news?

"So, the other night… Um, two nights ago," Elena said, casting a meaningful look at Blake before glancing away. "A couple of women came into the clinic for help, saying they'd been roughed up pretty badly."

Matteo's face darkened. "Shit. Did they report it to the police?"

"We gave them that option," Elena confirmed. "It's standard. We see quite a few domestic violence victims, both adults and teens, date rape victims, and other victims of assault. We have procedures in place to hook them up with counselors, social services, legal representation if they need it." She took a deep breath and looked Blake in the eye when she continued. "What's *not* standard is that these women stated that they were roughed up—slipped a drug in their drinks, then stripped, and tied up—by a dom here at The Club."

Drugged? Stripped and tied up against their will? At *his* club? The tension that gripped him was immediate and total. He heard Matt suck in a breath and saw him sit up straighter, his hands gripping the arms of his chair. Slay, who had obviously already heard this nonsense, nevertheless gritted his teeth. Elena looked pissed.

"Impossible. Not a fucking chance," Blake said flatly, and Elena nodded.

"I know," she said calmly, and he understood she was angry not *at him*, but rather on his behalf.

Blake sucked in a breath. "Who are these women? I need their names, and maybe their images, so I can pull up security footage. Did they identify the dominants?" Without waiting for her answer, he turned to Slay. "Once Elena gets us that, let's find out when they were here and who they were with." See if there was an ounce of truth to the claims so they could take action.

But Elena shook her head. "Absolutely not. I'm not divulging their names to you."

"Pardon?" Matteo demanded, his eyes sparking.

"Exactly what *I* said," Slay agreed with Matteo, glaring at his sister.

Elena folded her own arms over her chest. "Those women come to *Centered* because there's an expectation of confidentiality. I won't break that."

"You *won't*," Blake repeated. "You won't help us figure out who's making bullshit claims against The Club? Or, on the razor-slim chance that something actually happened to them, figure out the perpetrator and see them prosecuted?" His voice was deadly soft in a way that made even Matteo flinch.

But Elena simply shook her head again, unperturbed. "I won't. For every woman who comes in making a bullshit claim—and yes, something felt off to me about these women even before they mentioned The Club, so there's no doubt in my mind that they're lying—there are a dozen women, maybe more, who come in because they've been abused, because they are feeling depressed, because they know that we will do our utmost to help them without judging or even telling anyone they were there. If I thought even *one* woman felt like she couldn't come to me because I broke confidentiality in this case, if even *one* woman had to stay in an abusive situation because she couldn't trust my discretion, I wouldn't be able to sleep at night." She leaned forward in her chair and swiveled her head, eyeing each of the men in turn. "And neither. Would. You."

Matteo shifted uncomfortably in his seat. Slay nodded in resignation. Blake... Blake had never been so goddamn proud of anyone in his entire life. The flare of annoyance he felt at being stymied faded to nothing in the face of it.

Three huge, muscled dominants and this little woman—*his* woman—stood up for herself and took shit from no one. He had to fight to keep a totally inappropriate smile off his face. Instead, he cleared his throat and said simply, "I get you."

Elena nodded, and as he watched, the fight went out of her. Her shoulders slumped and she smiled gratefully. It meant something to her that he agreed, that he understood.

Better and better.

"What I *can* tell you, after consultation with my boss," Elena continued, "is that when the women were offered the opportunity to contact the police, and offered legal counsel, they declined both. They said they'd already obtained legal representation, and they even provided us with the name of their representative, which is *not* protected information. A man named…" She grabbed her phone and clicked a few buttons. "Jeremiah Hakim."

Matteo frowned. He dug his own phone out of his pocket and began scrolling.

"Anyway," Elena continued. "The women indicated that Mr. Hakim would be contacting the police and filing a claim for damages in a few days."

"They can report it; I hope they fucking do. Let them investigate, because we have nothing to hide. But as to filing a claim, I don't know what they hope to gain," Blake said. "We have cameras on practically every inch of this place, we take every possible precaution, and nowadays we make even guests sign Waiver of Liability and Non-Disclosure forms. There is no way they have a case."

Slay shrugged. "Who the fuck knows? Why make a false claim in the first place, when you know you're making it harder for the women who are *really* being abused out there and are desperately trying to get someone to believe them?" He shook his head and sighed. "I'll give Mantle a call," he said, referring to Blake's old friend, a former task force agent who maintained strong ties to law enforcement and had helped Matteo's woman, Hillary, deal with a stalker a few years back. "Maybe he can look into this a bit for us. Give us a heads up if anything gets reported so we can jump on it."

Blake nodded, absentmindedly tapping his finger on the desktop. He was back in a state of suspended animation and it fucking killed him. He wanted to deal with shit proactively. He wanted a target.

"Bingo!" Matteo said, staring at his phone. "Jeremiah Hakim. I knew the name sounded familiar. I mean, how many lawyers named Jeremiah Hakim could there *be* in the Boston area in this day and age? Not exactly John Smith, is it?"

"Your *point*, Matt?" Blake interrupted.

"Right, right. So, you know Slay and I have friends with access to some, uh, information that's not common knowledge and is not always obtained with the assistance of a warrant?"

Elena rolled her eyes. "Super-secret-agent stuff. Got it."

Matteo rolled his eyes at her, but went on. "I've used those resources to dig into the Church of the Highest Prophet."

"Who?" Elena demanded, looking to each of the men for explanation.

Slay supplied it. "Some newfangled church that's been encouraging its members to send Blake hate mail, saying they need to shut down The Club. We're a bunch of degenerates, we're going to hell, blah blah blah. They've apparently taken it a step further and started monitoring us, taking pictures of the exterior of The Club... and of Blake."

Elena stared at Blake, concern written on her face. "They're monitoring... *you*? Like, a personal threat?"

Trust his woman to latch onto the same idea that had been nagging at Blake, but Blake shrugged easily, not wanting her to be alarmed. "I'm the face of The Club, honey, that's all."

If Slay or Matt noticed his use of the endearment, they didn't show it. He used the term casually, when dealing with their women, or even with Daphne. They didn't understand that he used it now in a very, very *un*casual way.

Elena nodded, and then her eyes widened. "Holy *shit!*" she exclaimed. "The protest! I completely forgot!" She smacked her forehead with the palm of her hand and jumped up from her chair. "The other day, the other *morning*, I mean. The morning of the day that these women made their claim?"

Blake nodded. "Calm down, Elena. Everything's going to be fine," he soothed. Meanwhile, he had to grab the edge of the desk with his hand, so strong was his urge to leap up and calm her down.

Christ. She'd better come to grips with things sooner rather than later, so they could get their relationship out in the open.

She kept her eyes locked on him and sucked in a breath. "That morning, I was running late to work."

Blake nodded. He remembered. Or, rather, MisterHaven did.

"There was a protest happening near the hospital as I was going in for my shift. Picket signs, angry yelling, the whole nine yards. I didn't have a chance to check it out, but I would almost swear that they were protesting The Club."

Slay let out a soft curse. Blake exchanged a glance with Matteo, who grimaced, as all of them connected the dots.

The women didn't need to prove their claims. They just needed to get them publicized. The false claims, the protests, the hate mail... all were part of a very, very well-executed smear campaign.

One that would be hard to keep from touching Elena, if they were to continue their relationship.

FUCK.

"It gets worse, boss," Matteo said. "Since we're already playing six-degrees-of-Jeremiah-Hakim, wanna guess what other notorious baddie is on Jerry's client list? I'll give you a hint—this guy was actually *represented* by Jeremiah the last four times he was in court and got off on technicalities every *fucking* time."

He pulled up a picture on his phone of two men in business suits walking down the steps of what might have been a courthouse. One was younger, Caucasian, whip thin, with dark hair and glasses. The other, was a heavyset, middle-aged Latino whose friendly smile made him look more like your friendly neighborhood tax accountant or overworked school principal than what he really was.

"I'll take 'Asshole Cartel Leaders We Hoped Had Gotten Themselves Dead' for $200, Alex," Matteo said in his best Jeopardy-announcer voice.

Slay shot him a furious look. "Funny, Matt. Except it wasn't *your* girl who was tossed around by a goon on Chalo Salazar's payroll."

Matt nodded and clapped Slay on the shoulder in apology.

Chalo Salazar. Drug dealing criminal with a penchant for young ladies... very, *very* young ladies.

That was all this fucked up situation needed.

"So Salazar is behind this," Blake surmised. "The whole smear campaign against The Club is his brainchild?" If so, the photo of Blake was not a shot in the dark, but a declaration of intent.

Matt shrugged. "Sure seems that way."

Slay shifted in his chair and reached up a hand to rub the back of his neck. "He took a hit publicly after his little lackey, Gary Levitz, was convicted of assaulting Alice. We weren't able to get enough to tie him to anything directly, but we were able to nail a couple of his best sellers and get them off the street, meaning he also took a *financial* hit. I was involved *very* heavily in both of those events. He's been laying low for a while, but it would not surprise me at all if the first thing he did when he'd gotten himself back on his feet was to come back at me, and through me, at The Club and Blake."

There was a thread of remorse in his voice that Blake had to address. "Hey," he said, pointing an accusatory finger in Slay's direction. "This is *not* on you, brother. Not remotely. You get me? And Jesus, so what if some Salazar-backed nut job wants to send me to hell? Your sister's been sending me to hell since the day we met and it hasn't worked yet."

Slay snorted.

Elena's eyes met Blake's, and he winked at her. She smiled widely, even as she shook her head at him.

"You worry about Alice," Blake continued, addressing Slay. "Allie and Charlie are your priorities, and you let *me* worry about The Club."

"Problem is that the fucker is so slippery," Matt said, scrolling through the information on his phone. "There's no way to get this information legally, and so there's no way to tie him to the church.

And the church, while annoying, hasn't done anything illegal yet, so..."

"So, we ride it out," Blake said.

"Or maybe not," Elena said slowly.

All heads turned to look at her.

"What if we don't *have* to prove anything? What if we play Salazar's game right back to him?" She looked from Slay to Matt, then her eyes caught Blake's and held. "What if we contact someone at *The Boston Star* about the information Matt obtained—all hush-hush, obviously, and not naming any super-secret-agent sources. And we could have *her* investigate things, and if she finds any evidence, she can write up what she learns! It might not be enough to convict Salazar of anything, but if we can suggest a relationship between a reputed drug kingpin and this Church of the Highest Prophet..."

"It would discredit the church!" Matt said, his eyes alight. "*Damn*. Good thinking, Elena. Easy to see who got the brains in your family, man," he added, nudging Slay.

Slay raised an eyebrow at Matt before turning to glare at Elena. "I don't like it. You say *someone* at *The Star*, but you mean Gretchen, don't you? Your college roommate?"

Elena nodded. "Yeah, but this is hardly a dangerous assignment for her, Alex. She's an investigative reporter. She's dealt with much worse than some corrupt church, trust me."

Slay huffed out a breath, and tipped his chin to Blake. "What do you think, boss?"

What did he *think*? He thought he wanted to take the woman, wrap her in a cocoon, and keep her carefully hidden away from anything that could hurt her... But as he was coming to understand, *that* would hurt her worst of all.

"I'm only going to contact her and pass on the same information I gave you. No more," Elena promised. "*Please*. Let me do this."

Blake stroked his hand over the stubble on his jaw, his eyes locked on hers, and he nodded, once. "One contact. That's it. If she gets back to you, or wants to meet, you come to us. *You will not take chances.* And, Slay, see if one of your *super-secret-agent* friends is interested in some side work," he said, enjoying the way Slay rolled his eyes. "I know you say that your friend is used to this sort of thing, but I'd feel better with a man on her," he told Elena. And then to Slay, "I'll comp his pay."

Slay nodded, pleased. But Elena looked as if he'd just given her the moon tied up in a bow. She was practically glowing with excitement, and Blake found himself needing to look away before he did something ill-advised... like bending her backward and *owning* her mouth, right in front of her brother.

"Jesus," Slay said, glancing at his phone. "I'd better go. I need to drop Elena and get home."

"Letting your girl play you, Slater?" Matt teased.

Slay grinned, not remotely put out. "Letting her *try*," he corrected, rising to his feet. "Makes it all the sweeter when I remind her who's in charge."

"Jesus," Elena gagged, rolling her eyes. "You're insufferable. How does Allie put up with you?"

"I make it worth her while," Slay laughed. "You'll see, baby sis. Someday in the distant future when you're ready to find a man." He reached out to tweak her nose.

"I bet you're right," she agreed quietly, her eyes on Blake. "I bet I *will* see." And she allowed Slay to usher her out the door.

Not two minutes later, he sent the first text.

MisterHaven: Behaving yourself, LanieLove?

LanieLove: Just sitting here in Slay's passenger's seat, not taking chances.

He snorted.

LanieLove: Hey, how did you know I was going to suggest that we go back to texting? I'm starting to think you're kind of a mind reader.

Right. More like he was smart enough to know that the best way to keep Elena off the church's radar was to keep her away from The Club, and from *him*, at least temporarily.

He sighed.

And he was also a man who knew that any dominant worth his salt considered his sub's needs and feelings before his own. If Lanie... *Elena*... needed time to come to terms with what he hadn't the smallest doubt they *would* become, he would give her that time. As much as it galled him, the best way to accomplish both aims, was to keep their relationship online-only for right now.

MisterHaven: I can't read everyone's mind, but I can definitely read yours. I bet I know what you're thinking right now.

LanieLove: LOL. Bet you don't.

MisterHaven: You're thinking about how it felt two nights ago when I bent you over my desk. How the wood felt against your cheek. The sound my belt made as I slipped it off. The way the air tickled your skin as you waited for it to connect. The sting, the pain, the rush of arousal. The way it felt when I slid inside you so, so deeply. The way we moved together. The way you cried out when you came...

One minute passed. Then two. He smiled. Just as he was about to type again, she answered.

LanieLove: Blake! You cheated! You knew the second I read those words, that's all I would be able to think about!

He grinned.

MisterHaven: I never said I wouldn't cheat, Lanie. Keep that in mind. If I'm going to be dreaming of you every night, I'm going to make sure you're dreaming of me. Every. Single. Night.

LanieLove: Gah! Enough! I beg you. I am sitting next to MY BROTHER here!! Changing the subject... NOW.

Blake imagined her squirming in the front seat of Slay's truck and laughed out loud.

LanieLove: So... have I ever told you how I got the name LanieLove? It was a nickname from my Grandma.

Nice attempt at distraction, baby, Blake thought, and he grinned as he replied, happier than he'd have thought possible three hours ago.

MisterHaven: No, you haven't. Tell me.

Blake found himself eager to hear her answer. He was eager for a lot of things where his LanieLove was concerned.

CHAPTER 6

Three weeks later, Elena stood in her shower, making the water as hot as she could stand it. It nearly stung her naked skin as she stood beneath the thrumming pulse of it. Work had been horrible. *Horrible.* The blessing and curse of being a labor and delivery nurse was that when it was good, it was *so* good, witnessing the miracle of life being ushered into the world, swaddling the tiniest of babies in soft blankets, helping their mamas feed them and hold them... but when it was bad, it was *bad*. When tragedy struck, it was gut-wrenching, and she'd seen it all.

She did not work at a quaint hospital in the country where happily married husbands and wives came in together and birthed rosy-cheeked newborns. She worked in downtown Boston, and working at an inner-city hospital brought its own pros and cons. Whereas they were chock-full of the most highly acclaimed physicians in the country, fully equipped to deal with any type of medical emergency with state-of-the-art equipment, they were also home to pregnant mamas of *all* walks of life. And sometimes, it absolutely killed.

Tonight was one of those nights. They'd admitted a full-term mother high as a fucking kite, escorted in by a wide-eyed taxi driver who'd already called the police. Child Protective Services had been notified, and a Boston trooper stood guard at the door with his arms across his chest, ready to book the woman as soon as her baby had been delivered. Labor had been grueling. They'd had to restrain the mother as she howled and fumed against them, and when, finally, they delivered her tiny, sickly baby, whisked away immediately to the NICU, Elena had been ready to hurl.

And now she stood in her shower, hours later, wishing that somehow she could wash away the anger and helplessness she felt at times such as these. Staying in the shower until the hot water began to cool, she quickly rinsed the conditioner out of her long black hair, and shut the water off. She nabbed a huge, thick purple towel made from Egyptian cotton she'd scored for a song at Marshall's, reveling in the luxurious feel of the terry-cloth on her hot skin. She dried her body before tipping forward, twisting the towel around her head, and slipping into the robe she'd bought that matched the towel. She sighed, feeling better already, as she sat on the edge of her bed and nabbed her phone. Three missed messages. She hadn't changed the contact in her phone yet, enjoying the fact that no one but she knew who *MisterHaven* was. She smiled as she looked at the texts she'd received while in the shower.

MisterHaven: How's it going, baby doll?

Elena was hardly what one would call a *baby doll*, but somehow coming from the big bear of a man who was decades her senior, it felt fitting. Between not going to The Club, and her crazy work schedule, she hadn't seen him as often as she'd have preferred, and she missed him. Her smile deepened as she replied to him.

Total shitty day at work, but I just showered and I'm feeling a bit better.

MisterHaven: Sorry you had a shitty day. Just showered? As in, you're still in a towel "just showered?"

She grinned as she replied. *Seriously? You ask me how my day was and the first thing your mind goes to is me, naked, in a towel?*

MisterHaven: Naturally.

Heat suffused her cheeks as she laid back, and her robe fell open, displaying her pink, cleanly-shaven legs. Biting her lip, she spread the robe open wider, barely covering her, and pulled it down over her breasts so her cleavage spilled out over the top. She snapped a selfie, satisfied it was one helluva pic. She grinned as she hit *send*.

Elena's heart tip-tapped a steady rhythm as she waited for him to reply. She jumped as her phone buzzed in her hand. It wasn't a text. He was calling, the name *MisterHaven* flashing on her screen. She swallowed hard. Was he going to lecture her for being inappropriate? Scold her for taking a risk and putting a lascivious picture of her *out there* where it could be intercepted by... hackers or something? She hadn't given it much thought until she saw his name pop up on her screen, and she could practically see his scowl, while he loomed over her, arms folded across his huge chest. Shit.

"Hello?" she said, her voice sounding oddly choked as she answered.

"Babe." God, she loved to hear him talk. His voice was a shot of whiskey, smoldering embers, well-crafted leather. She closed her eyes.

"Yeah?" she whispered. Is this how he'd begin his lecture? Her breath was coming in gasps, and she felt suddenly way too warm even though her robe had practically fallen off.

"Where are you?" he growled.

"On my bed," she continued in a whisper.

"Oh yeah?" he said, his own deep voice dropping. "Open the robe all the way, gorgeous."

Closing her eyes tight, she did what he said, slowly tugging so her robe opened.

"You shaved smooth, little girl?"

"Fuck yeah," she said, a slow, wicked grin spreading across her face.

"Touch yourself," he said, his voice taking on a hard, commanding edge. She threw her head back and gently stroked her folds. She gasped, shocked at how slick she was, her finger easily gliding over her clit. "Circle," he growled. Closing her eyes, she circled her clit as he said, an involuntary moan escaping.

"Oh, yeah, baby," he growled. "That's what Daddy likes."

Her stomach clenched. Fuck *yeah*. He continued talking in his low, gritty voice. "You've been a naughty little girl, Elena. So naughty. And now it's time you were punished."

Her eyes widened, and her hand froze. Was he serious?

"Close your eyes, babe," he crooned. "That's a girl. I've just dragged you into my office for mouthing off to me. Do I like mouthing off, little girl?" His voice took on a harder edge, and she stroked faster.

"No, sir," she whispered, grinning.

"Someone's gonna remember to watch her mouth every time she sits down for the next fucking *month*," he growled.

Faster, harder, her hand moved as his words went on. "I shut the door and lock it, and bring you to the overstuffed chair in the corner of my office. I sit down and haul you over my lap."

He paused as she stroked, the tension mounting, her hand shaking.

"You with me in this?" she whispered.

She heard his growl on the other end of the phone. "Fuck yeah." God, she'd never gotten a guy off on the phone, but the very idea of him with her, fisting his cock as she…

"You're gonna lose that skirt, little girl," he growled. "I'm pulling it off, and baring your ass over my knee."

Harder, faster, *fuck* she was gonna come.

"You're fighting me, but I'm stronger and you're not gonna win this. I pin your hands down, and spank you."

Her hips rose as she stroked, and his words kept coming, deeper, forced. "I slap your ass and my handprint brands you, my pink fucking handprint straight across your bare skin. You scream, but I keep at it, spanking your ass until your skin is burning, and you're begging me to stop."

He breathed low in the phone. "Toss the phone on speaker, grab your nipple with the other hand, baby, and *squeeze*."

"Oh my God," she whispered. She was going to die, she was so close, but she did as she was told, hit "speaker" and dropped the phone to the bed as she grabbed her nipple and squeezed, her other hand still working between her legs, bringing her to climax.

"Before you come, you ask me," he ordered.

"Please," she pleaded. "I'm ready *now*."

"Beg me."

"Please, Blake, fucking hell I'm gonna die if I don't come—"

"You come before I give you leave, I'll take my belt to your ass," he barked out, which only made it even harder to hold herself back.

"*Please*," she begged.

"Pump your finger while you squeeze your nipple," he responded.

Fuck. Shit!

"Gawwd," she moaned, listening to his own groans on the other side.

"I give you one final spank so hard you scream and lurch, but I hold you fast over my knee."

He paused.

"Touch your clit. Come for me, Elena."

Her world exploded as she came, her hips writhing beneath her own hand, heat suffusing her cheeks, moaning out loud as she heard his own groans on the other end of the phone. It was the most intense orgasm she remembered ever having, lasting so long she collapsed on the bed, her hand falling to the side.

"Good girl," he crooned. "What a very good girl."

She snuggled up on the bed and sighed contentedly, suddenly overcome with exhaustion, as she disengaged the speaker and put her phone up to her ear.

"You there, baby?" he asked.

"I'm here," she breathed, sighing. "God, I needed that."

He chuckled, deep and low. "Your spanking?"

She giggled in reply. "I could use that, too."

"You free tomorrow?" he asked. "I'm manning the floor tomorrow night. Most of the Dungeon Monitors are off. I know we've been asking you to stay away from The Club, but screw that. I'm tired of having to squeeze time in between your work schedule and mine. Park in the back and I'll come get you when you come. You'll be safe if you're with me. Are you cool with coming here? You wanted to get to know each other more."

She smiled. "Yeah," she said softly. "I miss going to The Club. I'd love to go again." What she didn't tell him was that it turned her on to see him, *her man,* in charge of the teeming BDSM club, and she *loved* seeing him on "his turf."

"I have to work until three, then I have a shift at the clinic," she said. It was somehow oddly satisfying to be talking about just normal, everyday things with him after they'd had epic phone sex.

"Come to me when you're done. Got it?"

She sighed at the command. She *loved* the command.

"Yes, sir."

"You sound tired, honey," he whispered. Her eyes felt heavy, so heavy.

"Mmmm," she said.

"Okay, baby. Put the phone down but leave it on, and go finish getting ready for bed."

"Mmm," she mumbled. She did not want to get up right now, when she was perfectly content and comfortable where she was, but the next words that came through the phone had her leaping out of bed to obey.

"*Now*, Elena, or that scene we just played out will happen for real when I see you tomorrow. You're tired, but you'll do as you're told."

She opened her eyes, and spoke into the phone. "I'll be right back."

Leaving the phone on her bed, she went back to the bathroom to take out her contacts and finish getting ready for bed. Opening her medicine cabinet, she reached for the bottle of contact solution, but realized she was out. Sighing, she looked under the sink for a spare bottle, and a box of tampons tumbled onto the floor. She picked them up, starting to shove them back into the cabinet, when she froze.

They'd been in there... for a few weeks. Or was it a month?

She raced back to her room, flicked her phone screen back on, and tapped open the app she used to track her cycle. No, no, no, no, *no!*

It opened up, bright red lettering at the bottom of the chart. *Seven days late.*

"Elena?" Blake's voice came through on the speaker of her phone.

"I'm back," she breathed. "Hey, I'm exhausted. I'm going to bed now, okay?"

"Yeah," he said. "Sounds good. You have a good night, honey. See you tomorrow?"

She gulped. "Yeah," she whispered. "Tomorrow. Night."

She disconnected her phone, laid back on her bed, and dragged her arm over her face. *God!* It wasn't possible. No *way.* How?

They hadn't used protection when they'd had sex in his office, but she was on birth control. She practically ran a women's *health clinic*, for crying out loud. How could she have gotten pregnant?

But even as she went through the thoughts of denial, the conversation she'd had a million times with women who came in her clinic ran through her head. "Is the pill effective?"

There's a small chance of pregnancy, even with regular, consistent use of oral contraceptives.

She loved being on the pill, because it regulated her periods, but until a few weeks ago, it had been months and months since she'd even been *with a guy.*

Could it really be that in the heat of the moment, with her bottom striped by his leather belt and his huge hands gripping her waist, that the one time they got it on in his office would be the *one time* she'd get knocked up?

Shit, shit, shit.

She knew she'd have to talk to Blake, but she was *not* going to talk to him until she'd taken a test. God! What was she thinking? She didn't *know* him, know him, like "let's have a baby together" level knowing someone. She just wasn't okay with freaking *him* the hell out when there was no need.

She felt her breasts. Not really tender. Was that a pang of nausea? No, not really. She put her hand on her abdomen, as if she'd suddenly feel a baby kick to confirm she was pregnant. No, she was overreacting. She wasn't nauseous, but she *was* very, very tired. No, the exhaustion came from having a long, shitty day at work, not from being *pregnant* for God's sake.

Didn't it?

ELENA PULLED into the parking lot of the clinic. The day had passed in a blur, and thankfully the majority of the work she did was "business as usual." She'd needed to throw herself into what was familiar and routine, because her mind was teeming with questions. As she'd held a tiny baby with a shock of hair, swaddled in a blanket in the nursery, she'd caught herself wondering.

Is it a boy? Is it a girl? Would he want a boy or girl? Then she'd caught herself mid-thought. God, she had to get a grip.

She'd placed the baby back in the bassinet, wheeled it to the volunteer who came every Monday, and marched herself out back to the main desk at the nursing station. Grabbing her water bottle, she'd chugged it down like somehow the cool liquid would chill her thrumming nerves.

He'd never had any children. Blake and his late wife had tried for years and finally given up. Would he be *happy,* at this stage of the game, to be bringing a *child* into the world? God! With *her?*

She'd grabbed a pregnancy test from the storage room, and snuck into a bathroom during her break. She couldn't take it anymore. She'd had to *know.* With trembling hands, she'd completed the test, flushed the toilet, washed her hands and waited. And waited. It had seemed like an eternity, but the test was negative. She'd tossed it.

Maybe too soon to tell.

She took a second test at one o'clock, during a coffee break, as if somehow two hours later her hormone levels would be ready to give her a positive.

Did she *want* a positive? She didn't even know.

At three, she took a third test, also negative, but three negative tests did nothing to alleviate her fears. If a woman had come to her at work or at the clinic, she'd tell her to wait, maybe her cycle was a bit off and another few days or a week before testing again wouldn't hurt anyone.

Ha! How easy that advice was to dole out when it wasn't directed at *her.*

She grabbed a protein bar from her bag, nibbled on it mechanically, and responded to Blake's text.

Yeah, yeah, I'm fine. See you in a few.

Off to the clinic, her phone buzzed one more time.

When you get here, march your ass straight to my office.

She frowned at the phone. *Yes, SIR*, she typed, hoping he'd question the level of snarkiness in her text. Even as she texted, she realized she was being a bitch, but what was a woman supposed to do when a *life-changing thing* might be about to happen?

She got to the clinic on time, and found it nearly empty, so she busied herself straightening up the paperwork they needed, when her phone buzzed.

You'll learn to watch your tone, honey. Oh for God's sake.

She typed a quick reply. *Whatever!*

She couldn't help it, as arousal pulsed low in her belly, even as she frowned at the screen. Another text.

Did you follow up with your friend at The Star?

She grumbled as she tidied up the pamphlets and slid them into the display case by the entryway. She had contacted Gretchen about Salazar weeks ago. What was taking so long with the investigation?

I'll follow up with her today.

She walked to her office, and on the way, nabbed two more pregnancy tests. Couldn't hurt.

She sat down, booted up the laptop, and searched out her email. It was the most reliable way to reach Gretchen, as she never knew if Gretchen was home or traveling. Taking a deep breath, she did her best to compose an email to Gretchen. Elena really had to work on compartmentalizing everything.

Hey! Just wondering if you got a chance to look into what we discussed?
Love ya,
Elena

Satisfied she'd contacted Gretchen, out of curiosity she clicked on the link for *The Boston Star*. She read through local political updates, local sports scores, and other headlines, until she came across an article dated just that morning.

BDSM Club under investigation after local church obtains well-supported petition.

She closed her eyes briefly before clicking open the article. Her eyes widened as she read. Had Blake seen this? She copied the link, emailed it to herself, closed her laptop, and went to the main entrance of the clinic. They were empty today anyway. Time to pay an early visit to The Club.

Her stomach twisted as she remembered Blake's earlier text.

March your ass straight to my office.

~

Elena nodded to Donnie at the door of The Club, then smiled to herself as the familiar blonde she was looking for came into view behind the bar. Though Alice had returned to school, she still took on occasional shifts at The Club, for which Elena was immensely grateful. Not having had a sister, her brother's girlfriend was a close second. She glanced quickly around. Damn Blake and his cameras. She was not ready to talk to him, face him, and face *whatever the fuck* he had planned for her. Fortunately, she knew that Blake was on the floor, and Alex wouldn't be around tonight, thank *God.* One less thing to worry about.

She sat at the furthest corner of the bar, and turned her back to where she knew the cameras would be trained, raising a hand to catch Alice's attention. Alice grinned when she saw her, and stepped quickly over her way. When Alice reached Elena, she bent down and kissed her cheek.

"Long time no see, girlie!" Alice said with a smile, sliding in to sit next to Elena. "How are things?"

Elena filled her in about passing her exam, how things were going at work, and explained that the clinic was faring well. As she talked, Alice frowned. "Honey, you don't look so good," she said. "You look pale, and like something's troubling you. You okay? You getting enough sleep?"

Elena was *dying* to talk to someone, and who could she trust more than Alice? She bit her lip. "If I talk to you, Alice, will you tell Alex?"

Alice frowned. "I do tell Slay everything. But if you need a little privacy, I get that. I mean, guys don't understand everything. As long as you're safe then yeah, I could see keeping it just between us girls." She smiled. "What's going on, honey?"

Elena sighed. "It's just something that needs to be kept quiet, *for now.* Not forever." If she *was* pregnant, then Slay would eventually know *anyway.*

Alice nodded encouragingly, which gave Elena the confidence she needed. She looked over her shoulder, around the bar, and then leaned in quickly before she lost her resolve. "I think I'm pregnant."

Alice's eyes widened, and her mouth literally dropped open, before she leaned in to whisper back.

"Whoa, have I been under a rock or something? Do you have a boyfriend I don't know about?"

Elena smiled weakly. "It was an, um, spur of the moment thing," she said, stopping herself before she said "one-night stand." She knew in her heart that what was growing between her and Blake wasn't just a *one-night stand.*

Alice nodded. "How late are you?" she whispered again.

Elena sighed. "A whole week."

Alice grimaced. "Well, honey, you're talking to someone who's been there. You know I have. And you also know I wouldn't change *anything*, and that my Charlie is the world to me." Alice's little Charlie was the most adorable little kid Elena knew, with a shock of blond hair like his mama, big eyes behind wire-rimmed glasses, and a huge, ready smile. He'd thrived being parented by both Alex and Alice together, and he called Elena "Auntie Elena." She adored him.

"I know," Elena whispered. "I'm just... I don't even know what to think."

Alice nodded. "I remember that feeling well. You take a test yet?"

Elena smiled weakly. "Five. In one day."

Alice snorted. "You know that's not gonna make the results come any sooner, right?"

"Well, fortunately in my line of work they're easy to obtain." Then she squeezed her eyes shut with a grimace. "You know, that's what makes me feel so *stupid.*" She opened her eyes and threw her hands up in the air. "I give advice all day to women about being safe, and using protection, and making good choices, and then I go and do this?"

Alice shook her head. "Do not even go there, babe. You *are* smart, and you know that even when you use protection, things can happen. They just do. And it's because you're smart that you're going to handle this the very best way you can." Elena nodded, and allowed herself to stop the self-deprecation, accepting what Alice said as true. Alice continued. "So… how do you feel about… the possible dad?" she asked.

How did she *feel* about him? She hadn't been prepared for the question.

"I can't say I love him… *yet*," she whispered, as tears welled up in her eyes. "But I… have never felt this way about a man. He's strong, and protective, and kind. He's smart and sweet, and *so damn sexy*. He's so good to me."

"Oh boy." Alice smiled, and cleared her throat. "Do I… know him?"

Elena swallowed. "Yep."

Alice blew out a breath. "Ohhh boy."

Elena laughed nervously. "Um, yeah." Anyone that both Elena and Alice knew would be someone involved at The Club, and if Alice knew him, then that meant *Alex* knew him, and both Alice and Elena knew her big brother was *not* gonna take kindly to a guy at The Club knocking his kid sister up.

"I like him, Alice, more than… well, more than any man I've ever known before. But we aren't ready for a baby, you know? I don't even know if we're ready for *us*."

Alice nodded. "God, do I know, honey. Of course I know. I was there, only I was trying to pull my shit together to get my high school diploma, and all I had were my super judgy conservative parents ready to throw me out. Look at what you have. An amazing support system with friends who love you, and a brother who absolutely worships the ground you walk on." She reached for Elena's hand. "And this isn't some loser you met at some random bar and don't know from Adam. If you know him from *here?* And I know him? And he's all those things you said? Then, honey, it's gonna be fine. It really will."

What she said made so much sense. Elena nodded. "You're right," she whispered. "I know you are."

It was at that moment she heard the deep familiar bass of his voice, and God, was she going crazy, but did she recognize the sound of his *step*? He was marching past her table when he caught her eye and froze.

"Alice," Blake said, with a chin lift, then, "Elena. When did you get here?" He folded his arms on his chest and Elena squirmed in her seat. God, he was total shit at feigning nonchalance.

"Little while ago," she said. "Had to talk to Alice a bit."

His gaze went from her, to Alice, then back to Elena. He didn't speak for a moment, then nodded. "Gotta hit the floor again. Meet me in my office in five?"

He was only being polite, making it a suggestion. Elena knew it was no suggestion.

She saluted him. "Aye, aye, captain."

His eyes narrowed, but he merely nodded and stomped away. Elena sighed, turning to Alice, and was unprepared for Alice's widened eyes and look of complete shock. "Blake," she whispered. "Holy *shit*."

Was it *that* obvious? Elena swallowed hard. "I didn't say it was Blake, Alice," she hissed.

"You didn't need to," Alice whispered back.

Elena sighed.

She sat in silence for a moment before Alice spoke up again. "Alex thinks the world of him, Elena," she whispered. "I can count on one hand the people he loves like Blake. Actually, make that one *finger*, and that man is already practically married and has a kid."

Matteo, Alex's military brother and best friend, was the only man Alex trusted like he did Blake. Elena knew this. But still. She didn't know who she was more nervous talking to, Alex or Blake.

"Babe?" Alice said gently. Elena nodded. "Blake said to meet him in five minutes four minutes ago. And I can attest from personal experience that with guys like him? He's keeping an eye on that time."

Elena smiled, getting to her feet, and nodded. "You've got it," she said. "Thanks, Alice."

Alice gave her hand an impulsive squeeze. "You're gonna be fine, honey."

It seemed Alice assumed Elena was ready to go tell Blake *now*.

Uh-uh. No way, no how.

But what Alice didn't know wouldn't hurt her.

ELENA KNOCKED on Blake's office door, and heard the deep, raspy, "Come in," down to the tips of her toes. She pulled the strap of her bag up higher on her shoulder, took a deep breath, and walked in the office.

He was sitting at his desk looking at all the security feeds when she entered. He nodded absentmindedly and gestured for her to take a seat. He paused and glanced at a clock on the wall. "Cutting it close," he said.

She nodded, as he looked more closely at the screen.

"Glad I got a firsthand look at the dungeon today," he muttered. "Wanted to see for myself we were following protocol."

"Were you?" she asked.

He turned to her with a scowl. "Fuck yeah, we were," he said. "Any dominant who comes in here and doesn't follow protocol answers to *me*."

She nodded, her mouth suddenly going dry at his "*answers to me.*" Blake ran a tight ship, and it was why lifestylers flocked to his club. It was safe, and drew a dedicated clientele who knew what they were about. There were people new to the scene, and people just exploring, but everyone was kept to high standards.

Blake put a small box on his desk and took out an X-acto knife, sliding it through the packing tape along the edge. "Tell me about your day, sweetheart," he said before he lifted his eyes to hers. "I want to hear about it before we talk about your tone of voice on the phone." He held her gaze for a beat, before focusing on opening the box. She felt the power of that look, and shifted on her seat, already feeling the need for him build low in her belly. Didn't help that she'd fallen asleep having climaxed at his command, and woken up after vivid dreams, only to replay the night before.

Did pregnancy make people horny?

She licked her lips, and watched as he removed bundles of rope from the box.

"Oohh," she breathed. "Is that for bondage?"

He quirked a brow. "No, it's for tying my luggage to my roof when I go on vacation in the summer."

She *humphed* at him, which just earned her a grin, the delicious wrinkles around his eyes warming her with a little pitter-patter of her heart, as he continued to unpack the box. "Hell yeah, this is bondage material. Hand-dyed organic cotton, hemp in its natural form, synthetic Zen." He placed various bundles on his desk, then removed one with care, reverence in his voice. "And some high end tossa jute for my personal stock. We don't keep this at The Club. Awesome stuff, but way too pricey."

"Gotcha."

Personal stock? Her heart positively stuttered.

"You were telling me about your day," he reminded.

"Oh. Right. Okay, so, the shift at the hospital was pretty routine, which thank God was the case because the day before sucked like you wouldn't believe." He nodded, piling the rope together as he broke down the box and neatly folded it.

"Delivered two sets of twins, both doing fine, then headed to the clinic, but it was dead there, so I came here early. Really nothing to talk about." *Oh, except the fact that I might be pregnant with YOUR CHILD.* She took in a shaky breath, hoping he didn't note her rising nerves.

"Is that all?" he asked, as he put the knife back in a drawer. She nodded.

He pushed his chair back from the desk, and patted his lap. "Come here, Elena," he said softly.

She rose, his soft command making the need between her legs intensify. God, she was hopelessly addicted to this man. She walked slowly to him, her eyes roving over him. He wore his signature blue button-down shirt and jeans, the crisp white cotton of his t-shirt peeking out at the very top. His beard was full and neatly trimmed, the flecks of gray making her heart thrum a steady beat. The gray around his temples accentuated the stark blue of his eyes... and those *eyes*. So full of passion, kindness, and the sternness of an experienced Dom. When she stood within arm's reach, he took her by the waist, and pulled her to sit on his lap. It felt nice straddling his lap, and her arms instinctively encircled his neck.

"That's it, baby," he whispered. "Such a normal day, then why were you short with me on the phone?"

"Just a lot on my mind," she said softly. God, she loved the strong, woodsy smell of him.

"Lot on your mind?" he asked. "I get it, but do you think that's reason to be snarky with me, even in a text?"

She shook her head, the desire to push him away, or mouth off, or defy him in any way, suddenly evaporating. She wanted to tell him everything. *I could be pregnant with your baby... our baby.*

I'm scared.

His fingers threaded through her long hair, wrapped around the base of her neck, and tugged, lifting her face. His mouth met hers, softly but possessively. Sitting upon his lap with the tingle of her hair being pulled, the kiss aroused her like no kiss ever had. His lips moved softly, then firmly, his tongue meeting hers as she squirmed upon his lap. He pulled away and whispered in her ear. "Do you need a spanking, Elena? Do I need to take you over my knee? Would that help you let go of what's on your mind?"

She swallowed. Hell, yeah, she needed a spanking. She wanted to be tied up, spanked, then fucked, in that order. Between working as nurse at the clinic and hospital, and being a frequent participant at The Club, she well knew that even if she was pregnant, with certain precautions in place, she could partake in most scenes. She yelped as his hand connected with her ass with a sharp spank. "I asked you a question, little girl, and when I ask a question, I expect an answer. Do you?"

"I think I do," she breathed. But as he leaned in to kiss her once more, the monitor on his desk buzzed.

Swearing, he hit a button. "Boss, back-up needed in the front bar," came the voice.

"I have to see to that," he said with a groan. She nodded, getting up off his knee, as her phone buzzed.

"No worries," she said. "I'll wait here."

He nodded. "You don't leave here, got it? When I come back, we'll talk."

He leaned in and gave her a deep, parting kiss before he left. She sighed as the door closed. God, she wanted him.

Her phone buzzed again, with an email notification.

Hey Elena,

Got your email. Sorry it's taken me so long to reply, but I've been researching. Got some info you'll want. Meet me this week for lunch? Shoot me a call.

Gretchen.

SHE SMILED TO HERSELF. It would be great to get in touch with Gretchen, and maybe, just maybe, what Gretchen had to tell her would keep her mind off all things Blake.

CHAPTER 7

"Hey," Blake said, stepping out of his office and lifting his chin in greeting to Donnie, who was already making his way down the hall. "Trouble at the front bar?" It figured that the one time Blake hadn't kept his eyes on his security feeds was the one time he was called to handle an incident.

"Yah, sounds like it," Donnie said, running a hand through the mop of sun-streaked blond hair that made him appear more like a California surfer boy than a hardened kid from Southie, at least until he opened his mouth. "I was down in the Red Room, but Jace called me to come up. Said there was a *situation*. He called you, too?"

Blake nodded, falling into step with the other man as they headed towards the front entrance.

"We're about due, eh?" Donnie continued. "Haven't had a fight or a security issue in a month. Was starting to get a little bored around here, waiting for something to happen. I'm ready to crack some heads." He jokingly pounded one fist into the palm of the opposite hand and chuckled.

Blake rubbed his chin thoughtfully, but didn't reply. Donnie was right, it *had* been quiet recently. Unfortunately, as far as Blake was concerned, it wasn't a joking matter.

Attendance at The Club was down. It might not have gotten to the point where the bouncers, the part-time Dungeon Masters, or the waitstaff had noticed a significant dip, but when Blake looked at the weekly revenue totals for the past month, the downturn was fairly obvious. Over the last few weeks, having The Club at capacity was the exception, rather than the rule. And he didn't have to look any further than the front page of today's *Boston Star* to know who to blame for the change.

Chalo Salazar and the Church of the Highest *fucking* Prophet.

Discretion was the hallmark of any successful BDSM club, and The Club was no exception. Over the years, Blake had devoted untold effort and a shit-ton of money to security upgrades, ensuring that his members' privacy would be protected. He had never gone for any of the quick-but-risky advertising methods he'd seen others try, like hosting open-houses, or even advertising their location in kink-friendly publications. And he'd *never* allowed his members to fudge the definitions of safe, sane, and consensual as so many fly-by-night clubs (*Club Black Box* sprang to his mind) had done, in the hope of drawing a larger crowd. Instead, The Club's reputation had spread slowly, by word of mouth, as a place for well-regulated, *discreet* kink.

But thanks to the ongoing smear campaign, The Club was now a household name, and the front entrance was monitored by a small band of protesters at random hours of the day.

Goodbye, anonymity.

Though neither Blake nor Slay's crew had been able to prove a direct link between Salazar and the church, Blake could see that asshole's fingerprints all over this debacle. From what Blake knew of Salazar, this kind of underhanded vengeance was totally his style. And it was the only way Blake could account for the way the church's protests against The Club had morphed over the past few weeks from some fire-and-brimstone-type hate mail to a far more incisive, sophisticated, and *personal* attack.

The church's initial *"Shame on you, sinners!"* spiel apparently hadn't made much of a ripple—not a shock in a place as proudly liberal as Boston—so it appeared they'd decided to change direction. Now, they were trying to frame BDSM as a social justice issue rather than a moral one, and were inciting the masses to protest. Which pissed Blake *right the fuck* off.

Not the protesting part—God knew, Blake had served his country so that people would have the right to assemble peaceably, to air their grievances in an open forum. But he'd be damned if he'd ever condone an organization using misinformation and inflammatory language to incite protesters for their own gain. And that was exactly what the church had done.

Thanks, no doubt, to Salazar's money, the church had taken out expensive full-page ads in *The Star* two Sundays in a row, describing what went on behind The Club's doors as "exploitation," "cruelty," and "abuse," language not even the most hard-hearted SOB could ignore. They'd gotten hundreds of people to splash twisted "facts" all over social media, calling Blake a "deviant" and submissives "victims." And it seemed that they'd successfully made The Club, *his* club, a poster child for every horrifying story of kink-gone-wrong that they could dredge up… or *fabricate*, as he was all-but-certain was the case with the two women who claimed to have been assaulted in one of The Club's dungeons by an unidentified dom.

Now, it seemed like almost every concerned citizen in Boston, from rosary-toting grandmas to fresh-faced college students, had taken a turn holding a placard out in front of The Club, or signing an online petition.

He didn't blame them for being outraged. They were simply directing their outrage at the wrong target. And as soon as he could *prove* the connection between Salazar and the church, he'd show them what the correct direction was.

In the meantime, his little PR problem was becoming a legitimate business concern. And with Salazar fanning the flames, he doubted that it would be going away anytime soon.

So much for his idea that he'd get things sorted quickly so he and Elena could focus on their relationship. He'd admit, getting to know her better through their texts and phone calls over the past few weeks had been pretty damn sweet. He'd been able to dom her, to keep tabs on her, to make sure she was taking care of herself at all times. More than that, he'd gotten to know her as someone other than Alex Slater's mouthy little sister, or the leading lady in every one of his sexual fantasies. He'd confirmed a truth he'd long suspected—that the biting humor and sassy attitude he loved hid a core of absolute goodness.

But God in Heaven, he was lusting after the woman like a fucking teenager. The first thing he did in the morning was reach for the phone to check his text messages. The questions she asked during their phone conversations, about rope bondage and implements and total power exchange, fired his imagination like nothing he could remember. And damned if he hadn't gotten himself off *twice* this morning just reliving the sound of her moan as she'd come for him on the phone last night. If he didn't get to fuck his girl again soon, there'd be hell to pay.

Blake took a deep breath. *One problem at a time*, he reminded himself.

He and Donnie approached the doorway that led from the members-only main bar into the front bar beyond. The door between the two areas was usually left open, though at least one of Blake's men was always standing guard to ensure that only members and their guests were allowed into The Club itself. Tonight, the door was closed, with Jace apparently on the other side. And the commotion in the front bar was so loud that Blake could hear it, even through the exorbitantly expensive soundproofing insulation he'd had built into the walls. It sounded like... chanting?

He and Donnie exchanged a look.

What the actual fuck?

He pushed open the door, and stepped into chaos.

Dozens of women and men—most of them Elena's age or a little bit younger, were packed around tables and crowded around the bar, chanting "Sexual Assault is Not Sexy!" He noticed a man in the back sporting a white t-shirt with bright-red lettering that said, "Partnership Not Patriarchy!" And near the front, sat a woman holding a baby, who sported a onesie saying "Don't Abuse My Mommy!"

Christ.

"Is that a, um…" Donnie stuttered, eyes wide as he caught sight of the child.

"A baby? Yeah, bud." He clapped the bouncer on the shoulder and asked wryly, "Still feel like cracking heads?"

Donnie turned to give him a disgruntled look.

Meanwhile, across the room, a pair of women were screaming at Jace and Vickie, who were barricaded behind the bar. Vickie, who had worked at The Club for years, and had been a waitress at a biker bar frequented by Hell's Angels for years before that, looked absolutely petrified as a protester leaned over the bar and hurled obscenities at her, while another took pictures with a cell phone. Jace, who had taken a position in front of Vickie, stared grimly at the protesters, clearly uncertain of how to handle this situation.

Blake didn't blame the man. He and Donnie had come out here to deal with a couple of drunks, or maybe a curious person who'd wandered in off the street and wouldn't take no for an answer from Jace. But a horde of protesters *inside* the bar? Yeah, that was a new and extremely unwelcome development.

"Jace," he yelled, his deep voice booming through the crowd. "Get Vickie out of here. Take her back to the break room and hang tight until this is settled."

Jace nodded and grabbed Vickie's arm to lead her out from behind the bar, through the crowd of protesters, and into The Club.

Blake stood aside to let them pass, and muttered to Donnie, "Okay, I've seen enough. Call the cops. I'll wait here."

But apparently Blake had already drawn attention to himself, because a man in the back shouted, "It's *him!* The ringleader! Master Blake!"

Blake folded his arms over his chest and gritted his teeth, though a sick feeling churned like acid in his gut. *God.*

He supposed escalation was inevitable. But how many of his employees' identities were known? How far would the protesters go? He made a mental note to discuss personal security with every member of his staff, so they could protect themselves and their families. And of all the nights for him to invite *Elena*...

"He looks just like in the picture online! *He* is the one who roughed up those two girls last month!" someone else cried.

This was so stunning, Blake felt his jaw drop. Was that Salazar's plan? Was he now going to have Blake implicated in a crime?

"Stop the innocent act!" a man in the crowd bellowed. "It's all over the internet! We know what you do to women, you and your *club*! This isn't the type of community we want our kids to grow up in!"

"You beat women, you control them, you manipulate them," another woman added. "'Dominant' is just a fancy word for *misogynist*! You prey on women who have no self-esteem!"

It wasn't the first time Blake had heard an accusation like that about the lifestyle, but it was the first time it had been hurled at him directly. And he couldn't give a shit what they believed about *him,* but then he thought of the strong, confident submissives he knew—Heidi and Hillary, Tess and Allie, John and Daphne, his Josie... and his Elena. Even knowing that it would do no good, he couldn't keep silent.

"I suggest you do some research, if you truly believe that," Blake said grimly. "Not only are you factually wrong in your assumption that all dominants are *men*, thereby invalidating the experiences of female dominants everywhere, you are fundamentally wrong about what dominance and submission means, and where the ultimate control of a healthy dom-sub relationship lies."

The crowd seemed to pause, looking amongst themselves, as though they hadn't expected a rational response. Had they expected him to lash out? Or perhaps to come out clothed in some Fred Flintstone-esque caveman ensemble and grunt at them? He rolled his eyes.

At the front table, the baby took advantage of the sudden silence to crow loudly, waving his chubby hands and grinning a gummy smile directly at Blake. For half a second, Blake felt his lips twitch.

"You can't expect us to believe the word of the most notorious dominant in Boston!" a woman at the next table barked, fixing him with a glare that might have singed the eyebrows of a lesser man. "You *beat* those girls!"

Blake shook his head. *Nope.* He certainly wasn't going to convince anyone here. But before he could say a word, an all-too-familiar husky voice called out from behind him.

"So, where's the police report!"

He knew that voice. He'd fantasized about that voice.

Oh. Fuck. No.

"If you all truly believe he's committed a crime, why hasn't he been arrested?" the voice demanded.

There were only a couple of times in his life when Blake could recall feeling an absolute disconnect with reality, as though he couldn't force his brain to believe what his eyes and ears were telling him. The first time had been after a three-day sleep-deprivation military training back in the day, when he'd started having hallucinations. The second had been thirty years later, when Josie's doctor had looked at them seriously and spoken the words, "Cancer. Metastasized. Terminal."

The third time was happening right this second.

His woman, his *Elena*, could not possibly have just walked herself out into a crowd of protesters armed with cell phone cameras, could she? After he'd taken every precaution to keep her out of the public eye, to keep her safe, for the past month?

Once again, the entire crowd seemed to still, and all eyes in the room turned to focus on the newcomer, including Blake's.

She looked like an avenging angel. That was the first thought that entered his mind. Her black hair tumbled down her back, untidy from when he'd run his fingers through it just a few minutes before. Her face was set in a mask of cold fury, and her dark eyes seemed to shoot sparks of rage at the assembled crowd.

Which, hand to God, was not one-tenth of the rage *he* felt, watching her endanger herself this way.

"I cannot believe that mature, socially conscious people in this day and age have dragged themselves, *and their babies*, out here to protest the way that other people *choose* to have sex!" Elena continued, glaring at one woman after another, in turn, but avoiding Blake's gaze entirely. "If I were gay or lesbian or transgendered, would you care who I had sex with? If I *chose* to paint myself from head to foot with tattoos, wouldn't you all tell me I had a right to do what I wanted with my own body? What in the *world* makes you think I need you to save me from myself? What makes you think you can make decisions for me when you don't even know me? Who says you can protest my personal choices just because you don't agree with them?"

The protesters gaped at her. The one holding the smiling baby in the front row spoke up. "But two women were beaten here at The Club. They said they're filing a civil suit!"

Elena snorted. "They can *say* all they like, but no paperwork has been filed. And the police investigation was closed within a day."

The protesters began muttering to one another and typing rapidly into their smart phones, perhaps in an effort to confirm Elena's statement.

Blake couldn't care less what *they* were doing. He turned and took a step towards his woman, and watched as her gaze met his. Her eyes were wary but defiant, telling him that she'd known exactly how much she'd provoke him by walking out here tonight, and she'd decided it was worth it.

He was proud and *fucking pissed* in equal measure, his blood pumping through his body like molten metal, setting every nerve ending on fire. He was gonna blister her ass so thoroughly that sitting comfortably would be nothing more than a pleasant memory for the next few days. And then he was going to kiss the shit out of her.

But first, he was going to get her the hell out of here.

He muttered, "Enough," and placed his hand on her elbow, blocking her from most of the crowd.

She pressed her lips together and looked up at him. "Blake, I—"

"Oh, there'll be plenty of time for explanations and excuses, baby," he assured her, giving her a smile that was anything but friendly. Then he leaned closer to whisper in her ear, *"When you're over my knee."*

She swallowed, licked her lips, and nodded.

Then before he could shuffle her back towards the door, which he saw was now standing open, despite being blocked by both Jace *and* Donnie, Elena shifted her weight to one side and leaned around him.

"The allegations are total bullshit!" she called to the crowd. "And I suggest you check your facts before you allow yourselves to be riled up. You might be surprised to find that the person bankrolling this whole smear campaign is actually a drug dealer by the name of... *mmmph!*"

Blake reached out a hand and covered her mouth before she could speak the name. He whirled her around and frog marched her three steps over to the door and into the cool quiet of The Club.

"Blake," Donnie said in a low voice. "Police are on the way. I'll call you when—"

"Handle it," Blake bit out, marching Elena forward, moving his hand from her mouth to her shoulder to steady her.

"Handle it? Myself? Usually it's you or Slay who..."

Blake paused and spared Donnie a glance. "I trust you, Donnie. If they wanna talk to me, you buzz me. But until that time, you take care of it. Yeah?"

"Yeah," Donnie said with a firm nod. "I've got it, boss."

"Good man," Blake said, nudging Elena forward once more.

"Blake, maybe you should—" Elena began, but Blake cut her off.

"Maybe *you* should take this opportunity to be *quiet*. Something you *should* have done *ten fucking minutes ago!*"

She was silent for the space of four steps before she opened her mouth again.

"But, Blake, honey, maybe—" she began again, breathlessly.

"Not. One. Word."

"Honey—"

They had reached his office. He pushed the door open with one hand and propelled her inside, closing and locking the door behind him then he turned away, and doubled over, bracing his hands on the desk.

Rage clouded his vision—rage against the church, against the protesters, against Elena herself for walking her ass into danger despite all their combined efforts to keep her safely out of the spotlight over the past few weeks—and he sucked in breath after painful breath in an attempt to control it.

Christ, had he *ever* had to struggle for control like this? Not for years, for decades, if ever. But then again, when had he been tested like this? No woman had ever been passionate enough, stubborn enough, *crazy* enough to defy him.

The thought of Josie flitted across his mind, and for the first time in a long time, he conjured her memory with no pain, no guilt. His sweet wife had been so strong, so gentle, so thoughtful. One day, not long before she'd passed, she'd taken his hand, as he'd sat by her bedside, and she'd begged him to take another submissive someday. Through her blog, she'd met several doms and subs who had lost their long-time partners or spouses, she'd told him, and she'd seen first-hand how hard it was for them to find fulfillment again, even when their grief had lessened, without that dominant/submissive bond in their lives. Knowing how strong his protective instincts ran, she'd hoped that someday Blake would find that connection with someone else.

He'd scoffed, of course. The connection he'd had with Josie, that perfect rhythm born of decades of growth and friendship and love, could never be replaced. But she'd just smiled her quiet smile and said she hoped he'd be surprised.

Blake imagined that Josie was right now laughing her ass off in Heaven, because he'd found that connection, all right. In the most unlikely of places.

Blowing out one final breath, he pushed himself off the desk and turned to look at the woman who'd somehow managed to get under his skin, to challenge him in ways he hadn't thought possible. She was standing two feet away with her hands clasped in front of her, knitting and unknitting her fingers as she watched him. She looked nervous.

She should be.

His rage had passed entirely, but his need to discipline her for what she'd done made his palms clench in anticipation.

"Shoes off, jeans down. You're going over my knee."

She inhaled a shaky breath... and to his shock, took a step away from him.

"Blake, we need to talk first," she told him.

"Elena," he warned. "You do not want to play this game with me right now."

"No game." She shook her head. "I just think we need to wait a minute. I know you're angry, but—"

"I'm completely in control," he told her truthfully. "I would *never* risk punishing you while I was too upset." God, did she think he'd punish her while temper was still riding him?

"No, no, I know you wouldn't," she assured him, taking a step closer and laying a placating hand on his forearm. "It's just that I don't think you should spank me. N-not now."

"Not... now?" He repeated the words slowly, like they were a foreign language. She was looking at him with a pleading expression on her face—not defiant, not scared, but weirdly hesitant. And for the life of him, *he had no clue what she was trying to tell him.*

He grabbed the hand that rested on his arm and yanked her gently forward until her chest was touching his. He wrapped one arm tightly around her waist, while the other sank deep into her hair and pulled... *hard.*

She cried out softly, but he ignored it.

"You walked out there, Elena. Into a crowd of protesters." His voice was rough, vibrating with tension. "Opening a Pandora's box that can never be closed. Did you take even one second to consider how thoroughly they could fuck up your life with just a few phone calls to your employer, let alone what could happen if your identity gets spread online?"

Elena glanced down. "No, sir," she whispered.

"And then, *then*, you delivered your little speech—"

"I meant every word of that," she said passionately, gazing back up at him, her eyes filled with tears. "They're crazy if they believe the things they're spouting."

"And what about the shit *you're* spouting?" he roared. "Jesus Christ, Elena, you were about to call out the most notorious drug dealer in Boston!"

"I watched the security feed after you left, and I couldn't let them say those things about you!" she argued, but he could see the realization of what she'd done written on her face, the remorse in her eyes, even as she spoke. "It was bad enough when they were making up things about The Club, but I wasn't going to stand there and listen to them tell lies about *you!* You're the best man I know, Blake! The best man I know!"

Her voice broke off in a sob as her tears spilled over, and Blake's arms came around her. *What the heck was this?* "Elena, honey—"

"I know," she sniffled. "You're right, it was stupid. I hadn't considered any of the things you just mentioned."

"I told you to wait here," he reminded her sternly, even as his hand rubbed up and down her back in a soothing way. "You know I would *never* want you to endanger yourself that way. Your safety is paramount. That's a *rule*. And you broke it."

"I know," she admitted again, lifting both hands to her face to wipe away her tears.

"Then we're fucking taking care of this. *Now*." His voice grew harder. "Donnie is handling the police. We will not be disturbed. Tomorrow, we are going to have a meeting—you, me, Slay, Matt. We're gonna get you security 24/7. We're gonna talk to our lawyers about what you need to tell your employers so you can get ahead of any shit that might come of this. But before we do any of that, young lady, before we figure out how we're gonna move on from this, we're going to *finish* it. You take your jeans down and put yourself over my knee immediately, or your punishment will double."

He heard her breath catch, saw her eyes flare at the *young lady*.

So she liked that just as much as he did. Good to know.

She took a deep breath, swallowed once, and began to speak.

"I can't," she said, holding up a hand when she saw his eyes narrow, felt his arms contract around her back. "*Can't*, Blake. Not *won't*. Because I *do* want to, really. I needed a spanking so badly before I even walked in here tonight, and I know, I can *see*, just how angry you are at me, and I know that a spanking would help clear the air before we figure out where to go from here, but... well... it's just that sometimes there are certain positions that aren't maybe the best idea, you know? A-and I don't have a lot of experience... or, you know, *any* experience really, but I've researched BDSM pretty extensively online and there are some concerns about maybe blood flow and restraints and the more hardcore stuff, or anything that would put me upside down for any period of time. But spanking would be fine, I'm almost positive. Just maybe not over your knee. A-and maybe not face-down at *all*, in the last trimester."

The words flew past him in a mad, hesitant, irrational, very un-Elena-like rush, but he caught onto the last word the way a man clings to a life preserver.

Trimester.

"Jesus Motherfucking Christ. A baby?"

He hadn't realized he'd said the words aloud until he saw the way Elena blanched, the way her eyes widened. "You... aren't happy," she surmised.

Happy? Was he *happy*? God, he didn't have the first idea how he felt.

He and Josie had tried for years to have a baby—a little boy he'd take to football games; a little girl he could dote on. But then the doctors had said that Josie couldn't have children, and Josie had said she wasn't interested in adopting. So, he'd moved Children from the category of *Things That Might Happen* to the category of *Things That Will NOT Happen*, and he'd tried his best not to think about it after that.

But now, with Elena... it seemed that God was giving him another shot. The image of a little girl with Elena's dark hair appeared in his mind and he sucked in a sharp breath.

Christ, but he wanted that.

He thought of his sweet Josie again. Yup, *definitely* laughing her ass off at the twists and turns his orderly life was taking.

He shook his head as a reluctant smile tugged at his lips, and he lifted his hand from Elena's waist to run it through his hair.

"I figured I was too old to have a kid," he told her, the hand at her back tightening even further, while his free hand cupped her jaw. He slid his thumb along her bottom lip and watched her eyes lighten as she read his smile.

She smirked. "Apparently not."

Yeah. Apparently not.

"How sure are you?" he demanded.

She took a deep breath and let it out. "Not very," she admitted. "My period is about a week late, which is really unusual. I took a test today, and it was negative, but it might just be too early in the pregnancy for the over-the-counter test to detect. I'm going to talk to the doctor at *Centered* first thing tomorrow morning and get a blood test done. I'll ask them to put a rush on it. We should know for sure sometime tomorrow."

Blake nodded. "I'll go with you."

"For a blood draw?" Elena smiled. "No, honey, you don't have to come for this one."

"Then you'll come to me as soon as it's done," he decided. "We'll wait for the results together."

Elena hesitated. "Here? At The Club? What about Alex?"

Blake shook his head. "We're gonna have to tell him about us. It's gonna have to happen."

"He's gonna lose his mind," Elena predicted.

"So be it," he told her.

Honest to God, that was not a conversation he was looking forward to, especially under the circumstances. Bad enough to explain to Slay that Blake had started a relationship with Slay's younger sister, a sister Slay was inordinately protective of. But to then explain that Elena might be pregnant? And, oh, by the way, that Elena had outed herself to a room full of protesters on Blake's watch? Yeah, *not* gonna be a good talk. Still…

"You want this, Elena?" he demanded. "You want to be with me? Long-term? Raise our baby together, if that test is positive?"

He held his breath. She was new to this. She'd never been in a D/s relationship before. And yeah, it seemed like she'd absolutely *thrived* under his dominance the last few weeks, and her curiosity and enthusiasm to experience the types of bondage and power exchange he craved had fucking *thrilled* him. But maybe it was too soon for her to know.

A few weeks ago, she'd needed more time. Did she still?

But she gave an emphatic nod, no hesitation. "Yeah. That's what I want," she said, and Blake smiled.

"Then Slay will get over it," Blake told her. "I'll make sure he does."

Her answering smile was so brilliant and warm that he had to kiss her. Her face tilted up, and his lips found hers. The kiss was soft, but it was loving, and so full of promise.

And then his goddamn desk phone rang, while somewhere nearby, her phone chirped.

"Later, you and I are gonna be alone in a room for a long time without a single phone," he swore, his lips still touching hers.

"No interruptions?" she asked, licking her lips in a way that meant she licked Blake's lips, too.

Christ. "I'm thinking *private island*," he told her, before reluctantly loosening his hands from her waist and stepping to the desk.

"I'm holding you to that, Master Blake," she sighed, as she slumped into a chair and started rooting in her purse.

"Yeah," he barked into the phone, his eyes still trained on his girl. Her kiss-swollen lips were fucking distracting.

"Blake," Matteo said, and the warning note in his voice had Blake turning around and paying attention. "What the fuck is going on at The Club?"

Blake scratched the back of his neck. Had Donnie or Jace called Matt? Shit. He'd hoped to keep this quiet until he'd had a chance to assemble the guys and have a meeting… or at the very least, have his long-overdue discussion with Slay.

"It's not a big deal, Matt. The protesters have upped the ante again. They had this group come inside—"

"Inside the front bar for a sit-in?" Matt finished. "Yeah, I know."

"Then you know I handled it. Had Donnie call the police to get them out of here. It's fine."

"You handled it," Matteo repeated.

"That's what I said."

"*You* handled it," Matt said again.

Blake was impatient. "Yeah, man, I fucking handled it. Tomorrow, we'll…"

"Cause, see, from what *I* saw, *you* weren't the one to handle it," Matt continued.

"From what you… saw?"

"Mmmhmmm. From the cell phone video I saw," Matteo drawled.

Oh, God. They'd posted a video online. Damn it.

"What website has it?" Blake demanded. "We'll contact them, get it taken down, before…"

"Wasn't a website, brother." Matt's voice was full of sympathy now. "It was Channel 13 Action News."

The breath froze in his lungs. The news? In the last few minutes… his eyes quickly flickered to the clock on the wall… okay, in the last *half hour*, he amended… someone had gotten a video of the protest on the *news*?

Matt said, "Listen, Hillie's here. She says to tell Elena that everything will be okay, and, uh…"

Matt broke off and Blake could hear a muffled conversation on Matt's end that sounded like *"Tink, I am not saying that… I said no… Oh, for fuck's sake, fine."*

"And Hillary says to tell Elena her hair looked great," Matteo relayed quickly, sounding extremely pissed off.

At any other moment, Matt's frustration would've made Blake smile. But not now.

"When I, uh, talk to Elena, I'll relay that message," Blake said noncommittally.

Matteo snorted. "Yeah, right."

"What's that mean, Angelico?" Blake demanded.

"Blake, if she's standing more than two feet away from you right now, I'll personally volunteer to clean the Red Room for the next three weeks. And I say *standing* because if you haven't spanked her ass into next week for that stunt, then the real Blake Coleman has been kidnapped by aliens!"

Matteo sighed. "I saw the way you looked at her on that video, man," he continued more quietly. "I saw the way *she* looked at *you*. Hillie saw it, too."

Blake was too stunned to speak. *Shit, shit, shit.*

He'd needed just one more day. One day to talk to Slay, to find a way for Elena to get ahead of the story and take steps to protect her job.

"Fuck. We need to do damage control," Blake muttered. "*Immediately.* I'll talk to Elena."

"Good. I'll call Slay and ask him to assemble his band of mutant superheroes."

"You mean his *super secret agents?*" Blake said flatly, remembering how Elena had referred to them.

Matt snorted. "Yeah, them. We'll meet tomorrow. And hey, on the off chance Slay hasn't heard anything yet, I won't say a word," Matt promised. "Later, man."

Blake turned to look at Elena, who sat cradling her cell in her hands, looking shell-shocked and a little bit pale.

"So, um… I meant to tell you earlier that Gretchen emailed," she told him. "I set up a lunch date for the day after tomorrow. I think she might have info about Salazar that she wants to give me in person."

Blake shook his head. "No. It's risky for you to meet with her now."

Elena scowled. "Not much riskier than it was before," she countered, shaking back her hair. "Salazar had to know that you'd figure out he was involved. I just confirmed it for him."

Blake sucked in a calming breath as a pulse of anger flared in his chest.

"*Way* riskier," Blake reminded her. "Because that plan was concocted before we thought you might be pregnant."

"I'm not walking a tightrope or strolling through a landmine course! I'm having lunch with an old friend. Salazar has no idea it's anything *but* that," she said. "And besides, now more than ever, we need to get this *finished*. We can't wait around while they mess with our lives."

Blake ground his teeth together. The hell of it was, she was right. He wanted to know whether Gretchen had managed to find something even Slay's men hadn't. Blake knew he was being overprotective, and he instinctively recognized that would only smother Elena. Wrapping her in cotton and keeping her locked up might make *him* breathe easier, but it wouldn't be in Elena's best interest at all.

"Fine," he gritted out. "Then I'll go with you, or one of Slay's guys will. Slay already arranged protection for Gretchen, but I'll make sure he gets someone else to cover you—"

"That's the other thing," Elena interrupted. "Hillie texted. She knows about the protesters and about… us. It's only a matter of hours until Slay knows, too."

Blake nodded and crouched by Elena's feet.

"I figured," he said.

"God, that spread fast, huh?" Elena breathed, pushing her heavy mass of hair back with one hand while she stared at the ceiling, blinking back tears. "Boy, when I mess up, I do it *thoroughly*. I really didn't think. I just… I was so stupid, Blake."

Blake took both of her hands in his, forcing her to look at him. Her hands were fucking trembling.

"You listen to me, Elena Slater," he said gruffly. "Everything is going to work out. We're gonna make sure you are safe and protected. And your brother… well, Slay is gonna come charging in here like a bull. He's gonna be loud as hell, and he's going to stomp around cursing my name, because I broke the bro code by hooking up with his sister."

He didn't add that Slay would be well within his rights to take a swing at Blake, too, and likely wouldn't hesitate.

Elena looked at Blake skeptically. "Bro code, huh?"

"It's a thing," he confirmed, giving her a brief smile. "But the point is, he's gonna do all that shit because he loves you, because he wants to make sure that the man you end up with is going to take care of you and keep you happy for the rest of your life."

She sniffled and nodded. "I know."

Blake lifted their joined hands to run his thumb over her cheek. He stared into her gorgeous dark brown eyes and saw his future written there.

"But by the time he leaves here, honey," Blake said softly. "He's gonna know that *I am that man.*"

Elena gifted him with a huge, elated smile... a second before she dissolved into sobs and threw her arms around his neck.

"You mean it?" she whispered.

"Yeah, baby," he told her. "Every word."

A second later, she pulled back and rubbed her eyes with her palms for the second time that evening.

"God, I'd better be pregnant," Elena announced. "Otherwise I'm gonna lose all my badass cred. I'm a fucking watering pot."

He straightened, then leaned back against his desk, pulling her to stand between his legs.

Blake snorted. "Baby, I hate to be the one to break it to you, but I don't think you had a lot of badass cred to begin with."

A lie, and they both knew it, but it succeeded in distracting her completely.

"That's what *you* think," she told him, wrapping her arms loosely around his neck and pressing her lips to his. "I happen to be kissing *the most notorious dominant* in Boston. I'd say that's pretty badass."

And despite all the shit that had rained down on them, and the shit that was yet to come, Blake wrapped his arms around his Elena, threw back his head, and laughed.

CHAPTER 8

*I*f Elena thought Blake was crazy overprotective and badass *before* he found out she might be bearing his *offspring,* his level of overprotectiveness now was damn near suffocating.

"Listen, Blake," she said, with practiced patience, as he tucked her arms in her jacket and spun her around to zip it up. "Honestly, I really can get myself ready to face the *biting* fifty-degree spring day." Her voice dripped with sarcasm, as fifty degrees in Boston was damn near time to pull out the flip-flops and hoodies.

"Didn't say you couldn't," he muttered in a husky growl as he finished pulling up the zipper and escorted her outside. "Just wanted you to let me do it." Her tummy dipped as she took him in again. His blue eyes shone, the wrinkles around the edges making her heart stutter. He nabbed her elbow, tucking her close to the building-side of the street, as he intentionally flanked her right side where the cars whizzed toward the busy downtown Boston intersection. "Careful, baby," he muttered, easing her over a crack on the sidewalk. She smiled to herself. It was cute.

It was also the first time they walked in public with each other, hand in hand, after her name had been plastered on the front page article of the *Boston Star*. Elena knew at this point Slay had been informed of what was going on between her and Blake, and she could only hope that Alice had somehow softened the blow. Slay was heading into The Club that night for a late night shift, and her stomach already churned knowing that she, Slay, and Blake needed to have a talk, and when they did, her older brother would very likely lose his mind. But right now she had bigger fish to fry.

The reason Blake was walking with her in broad daylight was because *first*, they were on their way to get some lunch, and *second*, this afternoon, she would receive the results of her pregnancy test and Blake hadn't wanted her to be alone when she got the news. Her phone sat like a hand grenade ready to blow as she waited for her coworker Nancy to give her the call.

Blake steered her past the big display of newspapers with The Club plastered on the front page, heading to a neighborhood Greek restaurant the locals loved.

"Okay, so I don't really get it," she muttered, enjoying the warmth of her hand in his as they walked briskly along. "Salazar sets his crazyass cronies onto you guys because of… what? Revenge? Jealousy? What exactly is he hoping to accomplish with this shit? And why don't you just call him out and sue his ass?"

A muscle twitched in Blake's jaw as he guided her to take a right at the corner. "Don't say his name so loud," Blake growled. "Jesus, Elena. The only reason I'm allowing you out like this in broad daylight is because I'm with you. You got that?"

"Jesus, Elena," she mocked. "Hey, are you packing a weapon or something?"

Blake gave her a sidelong look. "You've got quite a potty-mouth there, little girl. And *for your information*," he hissed, tugging her a little closer as a sketchy-looking couple walked past them, "*I'm* not packing a weapon, but the guy tagging us sure as fucking hell is."

"Potty-mouth, he accuses, while cursing in the same breath," she muttered.

He growled, actually legit *growled*, and for a moment she was glad she'd landed a temporary reprieve from his palm of steel, because he looked like he was about ready to tan her ass right there on the corner of Comm Ave and Main.

"Blake," she said, stopping just a few feet shy of the entrance to the restaurant. "Take it easy, okay? There's no need to worry."

His brows drew together as he released her hand and stopped walking, spinning her around toward him. He put both of his enormous palms on her shoulders. "No need to worry, baby? I've got the biggest drug lord in all of Boston trying to take down The Club I've poured blood, sweat, and tears into for longer than you've walked this earth. I've got my woman on my arm, about to find out if our lives are going to change forever. And I've got to face her brother, whom I love like he was my own flesh and blood, and tell him that I'm with his baby sister. And he knows what it means to be with *me.* He knows we don't spend our free time playing mini golf and drinking fru-fru coffee at the country club." He ran a hand through his sexy-as-all-hell salt-and-pepper hair and blew out a breath. "But I'm not *worried*. I've got this. *All* of this. What I'm *not* is nonchalant about all this shit."

She let her eyes roam over the muscles in his shoulders, which rippled under the edge of his sweatshirt before she stared into his eyes the color of dusk in winter, pools of dark blue that turned her legs to jelly. "It's okay, honey," she said, resting her hand on his bristly cheek.

"Elena," he said, as one hand lifted off her shoulder and curved around her neck. "No, it's *not* okay," he whispered, leaning in to her as he brought her forehead to his lips and kissed her softly. "But it will be. No matter what, I give you my word. I've got this." She closed her eyes against the rising swell of emotion in her chest. God, this *man.*

"Hungry, honey?" he asked.

She nodded as his eyes flitted behind her. "Then let's get some grub." He took her by the hand again, but as they approached the restaurant, her phone buzzed. A bolt of fear raced up her chest, and she froze, unable to follow him even as he tugged on her hand. The number on the screen was from the hospital.

"It's them," she whispered, suddenly stricken. "What do I do?"

His eyes crinkled around the edges, his voice low and soothing when he spoke. "Answer it, baby." She swallowed, forcing her voice to work when it seemed suddenly she was almost unable to. She swallowed a second time before she answered. "H'lo?" she croaked.

"Elena?" It was Nancy. Blake's eyes held hers as she nodded to him.

"Yes?" she responded, her voice sounding unnaturally high.

"I'm sorry, honey," Nancy continued, and Elena felt her heart sink as Blake's hopeful eyes met hers. "The test is negative. You're not pregnant, Elena."

Elena exhaled, her throat feeling tight while at the same time, guilt overtaking her as she realized that she was both disappointed and relieved. She shook her head at Blake, tears pricking her eyes as his face fell, barely processing Nancy's voice on the other end. "See you tomorrow?"

"Yeah, thanks, Nancy. Okay, see you then."

A click, she shut off her phone, and shoved it back in her pocket.

No baby. No squealing little, curly-haired cherub that had his daddy's eyes. No little girl to dress in frilly dresses and wide-brimmed hats and baby-sized Mary Janes.

"No baby?" Blake asked. She shook her head, her heart constricting as he reached to brush a tear off her cheek. Was she crying? She hadn't even realized she was.

"I'm sorry," she whispered, as he pulled her fiercely toward his chest, tucking her against him.

"No," he whispered. "There's nothing to be sorry about, honey," he said. "This just means no for now. Now, we do this right. I get you a ring. I get you a house. I face that big bear of a brother of yours." He paused, chucking a finger under her chin. "And I put you over my knee and give you that spanking you've got coming to you."

She laughed in spite of herself, and realized what a weight was lifted at the sound of his words. God, yes, he was right. He was so right. This wasn't the end. This was only the beginning.

∾

THEY WALKED in silence back from the restaurant, Elena toting a little white paper bag filled with baklava, the flaky Greek pastry layered with honey, butter, and walnuts Blake had insisted she buy for later.

"After we talk to Slay, you're coming back to my place," Blake explained in his low, husky voice, and as they waited at the corner for the walk light to flash, he leaned down, kissing her temple before he whispered, "It's time, baby."

Time for what? Her heartbeat thundered in her chest as she wondered what he had planned at his place. She thrilled at the chance to finally see where he lived, and knew in her heart that being taken back to his home, his sanctuary, the place where he and Josie had resided for decades, marked a decided change in their relationship. She swallowed.

What exactly did the most well-known dominant in Boston keep in his house? What awaited her? But before she could wonder at what the evening held, her mind reeled back to the present. They were only a block away from The Club, where Alex waited for them. She felt like she was a teenager, arriving home on the backseat of a tattooed, leather-clad boy's motorcycle after curfew, prepared to meet Daddy's disapproval. Blake had grown quiet as they arrived at the entrance to The Club. Fortunately, the protesters at The Club had momentarily called it quits after her tirade the day before, and they entered via the front door without an issue.

Donnie nodded to them as they entered, his eyes sympathetic.

"Hey," Elena greeted, and Blake gave him a chin lift.

"Master Blake, Slay's waiting for you," Donnie said, his lips twisting in a grimace. "I told him you'd be back, and he said he'd be waiting in your office."

"Thanks, Donnie," Blake said, stoically escorting her past the bar and toward his office at the back. He leaned down to whisper in her ear, "Don't worry about this, baby. This is gonna be just fine. Slay loves you, and I know how to handle him. Frankly, although I respect him as my friend, I don't give a shit what he thinks about us."

At his words, Elena suddenly felt a rising sense of injustice. "You know what?" she said, as they walked to his office, the sounds of those around them fading as the dark door loomed. "I agree with you. God, the overbearing ogre will have to accept that I'm a grown-up, and I make grown-up decisions. I'm with *you*. An hour ago, I'd have accepted the fact that I was carrying your baby. I'm fully prepared to pack a toothbrush and spend the night at your place, because *I'm with you*. Alex can fucking *deal*."

Blake groaned. "Here we go," he muttered under his breath.

She frowned, looking at him. "What?"

He grinned, his eyes crinkling around the edges. "You're stunning when you're pissed, you know that?"

She smiled back. "Aw, you say the sweetest things," she said sarcastically.

They stood hand-in-hand, right outside the office door. "Okay, babe," he said. "For God's sake, Elena, follow my lead, got it?"

"Yeah, yeah, yeah," she said, nodding. "Open the door already."

But Blake didn't. He leaned in and whispered in her ear. "Don't *yeah, yeah, yeah,* me, young lady." His breath tickled her cheek, his large, warm hand resting on her lower back. She swallowed as her nipples tightened, her pussy clenching with need as he continued. "Your 'get out of spanking free' card has expired. Pass directly to jail. Do not collect $200 dollars. I'm taking you back to my place tonight, and we'll deal with the past few days the way I prefer. Right now? You *really* don't want to push me. You get me?"

His voice was controlled, even, as she swallowed and nodded. "I get you," she whispered. "Now open the door already."

"Oh for fuck's sake," he muttered, rolling his eyes, as he twisted the doorknob and opened the office door.

Alex stood, leaning against the edge of Blake's desk, his massive arms crossed on his chest, his jaw clenched. His brown eyes positively bore through hers as Blake ushered her in. For once she wished Blake wasn't so chivalrous that he held the door open for her every time, because now was the one time she really wanted him to go in first. Her eyes flitted to the screens on Blake's wall, as she realized that they were still on. They were *always on*, and damn it if Alex hadn't seen their little exchange right before they went in.

Fuck.

Blake closed the door, removing his jacket, and nodding to Alex.

"Slater," he said in greeting, hanging his jacket up on a peg on the back of the door, then reaching for Elena's. He helped her out of it and hung it up next to his.

Alex merely glared.

Blake took Elena's hand and walked to his desk, gesturing for her to take a seat. She sat, watching the two men she loved more than anyone else in the world glare at each other.

Finally, Alex unclasped his arms, only to plant his hands on his hips and turn on Blake. "You gonna tell me what the *fuck* is going on, and why I woke up today to find my sister's picture plastered all over the *fucking* internet?"

Elena felt her anger rising as the full heat of Alex's fury was directed right at Blake. "Alex," she began, lifting a finger, but Alex stopped her with his palm raised.

"Do *not* talk to me right now, Elena," he growled. "I'll deal with *you* after I deal with *him.*"

She got to her feet, ignoring the warning look Blake shot her. "No, you will *not*," she began, but Blake cut her short.

"Elena, stop," he instructed. She met his eyes and saw the command there. Was she his submissive? Hell yeah. Elena sat. She *wanted* to let him take the lead here, even though her temper was rising.

Alex faced Blake. "You dom her now?" he said, his voice rising in anger. "You think it's okay to tell her what to do?"

Blake stood across from Alex, and something shifted in his gaze. Whereas before he looked calm, it now looked as if he'd made up his mind. He continued, ignoring Alex's fury. "Yes," Blake said. "I *do*. Because I'm a *dominant*, and you of all people should know what that means. It means I lead her. It means I take care of her. I make sure she's safe, and she takes care of herself, and that no harm comes to her."

Alex's eyes flashed as his hands flew off his hips and he took a step toward Blake.

"Don't you fucking tell me what a dominant does," he said, pointing an irate finger at Blake. "I know what a dominant does, and that's exactly why you'll stay the *hell* away from *my sister*, because you're old enough to be her fucking *father*."

Elena sprang to her feet. Forget Blake's warning to let him deal. Fuck letting them sort out their "bro code" transgressions. She was not going to sit idly by and let Alex rake her man over the coals.

"Lay off, Alex!" she hissed, taking a step toward them, and that was when all hell broke loose.

"Sit *down*, Elena," Blake growled.

But the second he did, Alex's fist shot out as he bellowed at Blake, "Don't you fucking dom her!" His fist connected squarely with Blake's jaw, and Elena heard the *snap* from the force of the blow as Blake groaned, knocked back.

"Alex!" she shouted. "Leave him alone!" She reached her hands out but Alex was rearing back to deck Blake again. His forearm knocked into Elena as she charged at him, pushing her backward while she uttered an "*oof*," falling thankfully into a seated position in the chair. Blake had recovered from the blow, somehow managed to block Alex's second swing, and shoved him backward so that Alex fell to sitting beside Elena.

"Enough!" Blake roared. "You almost decked your sister, asshole, and even though I deserve what I got, she fucking *doesn't*. Sit, Alex, or I'll defend myself and you don't want that anymore than I do!"

The two of them stared at each other, chests heaving.

"God, it's like some kinda sick pissing match, and I can't tear my eyes away," Elena muttered, which earned her a glare from both Alex and Blake. She pursed her lips and quirked a brow. "So? You gentleman gonna continue, or are we done here?"

"Brat," Slay and Blake said in unison, which made Elena snort, but only earned her further glares.

Finally, Blake lifted a hand, gesturing for everyone to calm down. "Listen," Blake began. "Honest to God, man, when I first started getting to know Elena I didn't know she was your sister."

"Bullshit," Alex muttered to himself, but Blake's blue eyes grew stormy as he fixed a stern gaze on Alex that actually made him squirm.

"Enough," Blake bit out. "God, man, *listen.*"

Elena swallowed. It was one helluva dom who could make Alexander Slater do what he said, and Alex's willingness to listen underscored just how very much Alex respected Blake.

"You listening?" Blake asked in a low voice, while his blue eyes continued to keep Alex riveted to his seat.

A muscle twitched in Alex's jaw, but he nodded.

"Good," Blake said. "Elena and I met online, and it was like some kinda miracle. Honestly, if we'd only known each other face-to-face, I don't think we'd ever gotten past sparring with each other in the bar and pissing each other off. But… well, we did. Elena used to read Josie's blog, and when I finally wrote a blog post letting Josie's readers know she had passed, Elena offered her condolences." Blake shrugged. "How was I supposed to know that the girl with the screen name LanieLove was the same girl who pissed me off at my very own club?"

Alex's eyes met Elena's, and Elena could only nod.

Blake continued. "So, we got to know each other. We wrote to each other. Texted. Chatted. I really liked her, and the feeling was mutual. The next thing you know, one day we were right here in this office, Elena was mouthing off to me as usual, and we realized that the people we were texting were the very same people we were facing." Blake shrugged. "What can I say? I liked her. I was in too deep. I'm not sure how things would've gone if I'd known from the beginning that you were LanieLove's brother." Blake's voice dropped. "You know I love you like a brother, Slater. I don't need to tell you that. Honest to God, I had no idea that I was..." he paused, meeting Elena's eyes, before he finished, "falling in love with your sister."

The only sound in the room was the soft humming of the light bulb fixture above them, as the room was soundproofed and the monitors had been muted. Elena felt her heart constrict in her chest as she met Blake's eyes.

Falling in love.

She smiled weakly at him, nodding, as she faced Alex.

"He's right," she said softly, her anger now gone. "Every word he says is the truth. I swear it, Alex. I had no idea the man I was... falling in love with was *your friend.* No idea. And then when I did find out..." she paused, her voice dropping, "it was too late." She swallowed, before she looked back at Blake. She lifted her head high as she met his eyes. "I was already in love."

Alex ran a hand over his face, closing his eyes. Elena's heart went out to him. She knew how worried she made him, how badly he wanted what was good and right for her.

"Alex," she said, reaching her hand out to his. "I... this wasn't what I'd planned," she said softly. "But it is what I *want.* Please hear me in this."

"I hear you," Alex said, shaking his head. "And I don't really get it, and it'll take some time to get used to, but I just want what's best for you, Elena." He looked to Blake. "Matteo and Blake are the only guys I know I'd trust my life with," he said. "It's not that I don't trust him. But have you two thought this through? What the age difference means for you if you... get married, and have kids and shit like that?"

Elena smiled at him. "Yeah," she said, with a wry laugh. "We've thought of that more than you'd know." She met Blake's eyes, and his were smiling at her. She turned back to Slay. "I know this isn't what you would've chosen for me. But honestly, Alex, you beat up every single boyfriend I ever had in high school, and by the time I hit college I didn't even *tell* you when I went on a date."

Alex's brows drew together. "I thought you just took a break from dating while you focused on nursing. You mean to tell me you kept shit from me?"

Elena snorted. "Uh *yeah*, Alex," she said. "A girl has to sow her wild oats without having her big brother breathing down her neck and threatening to kick the ass of anyone who so much as even tried to get a little tongue action."

Alex growled and Blake cracked his knuckles, but she went on. "The fucking double standards make me just about go cross-eyed. I mean, who ever heard of a *tattoo artist* who wouldn't even let his own *sister* get inked? Huh? Of course I had to hide shit from you!"

Alex frowned, and Blake growled, "You got a tat?"

She grinned, and wished she was chewing gum just so she could snap it. "Yup," she said smugly. "Three, to be precise." *And won't you love playing hide and seek to see where they are?* she thought as she looked at Blake.

Blake shot her a look back that said *Behave.* She merely grinned.

"*Unfuckingbelievable*," Slay groaned.

Elena just shook her head. "Listen," she said, sobering. "Sometimes you can't predict the future. You don't know who you're gonna meet, or how things will turn out. You don't know... who you'll fall in love with."

Slay nodded, as Elena looked back at Blake. His eyes had grown softer, and she suspected he was remembering the years he'd spent with Josie. He'd likely never envisioned the day she'd be gone, let alone looking to start all over again. "Sometimes you just don't know how things are really meant to be until they happen," she said, her voice dropping to a whisper.

"Ain't that the truth," Blake said, blowing out a breath.

Alex looked from Elena to Blake and back again, and finally, he nodded—one brief nod, but Elena knew what it meant. Alexander Slater was a Marine, a dominant, a man who knew what he wanted and would fight to the death to defend the honor, safety, and integrity of those he loved. When he accepted the veracity of a situation, he gave his word. Elena felt a lump rise in her throat as she sat between the two men who loved her.

Alex's eyes went back to Blake. "You gonna keep her outta the fray while we sort this shit at The Club?"

"Hell yeah," Blake said. "She's not coming back here until the air is totally cleared. Got a man tagging her at all times, and I'll be keeping a close watch. You have my word."

"But—" Elena began, but Blake cut her short with a hand raised in her direction, and a stern glare that made her close her mouth.

"No. I'm putting my foot down about this, and that's *final*."

She knew it wasn't for show and that he meant every word, but still, she couldn't help glance at Alex, who nodded thoughtfully. "Damn right," he said. "You do what he says. He's the one who owns this place, and now that you're with him, there's nothing here for you anyway."

He crossed his arms. She looked from one to the other, both implacable and stern, and she knew she wasn't gonna win this round.

"Fine," she mumbled.

They both grinned, and as they did, her heart soared. They had her back, and it would all work out.

"You taste like honey and butter," Blake said, his low voice in her ear causing her nipples to harden. She was straddling his lap on the leather couch in his living room, having just polished off the last bite of baklava, and they were celebrating the evening alone.

"You taste like masculinity and sex," she countered, running her fingers around the back of his neck and drawing his mouth closer to hers, as he growled in her throat and tightened his grip on her ass. "I fucking *love* it."

"You swear like a goddamned truck driver," he bit out, leaning his mouth closer to her ear and taking her lobe into his mouth with his teeth.

"No shit," she responded, pulling back and meeting his eyes. "What are you gonna do about it, old man?"

"Naughty little brat," he growled, and she shrieked as his hands went to her top, yanking it up, nimbly unfastening her bra, before his hands found her nipples and squeezed. "You really don't want to test me, Elena," he said, sobering, his voice dropping as his eyes narrowed. He twisted his hands, and she braced herself. The sharp bite of pain faded to a tingle. "You'll do as you're told, little girl," he said, his smoky voice like whisky on ice, brisk but biting. "I'm not shittin' around with your safety. And there's a limit to how far you can push me, Elena. I don't expect meek and mousy from you. No, baby, that isn't you, and I get that," he said, his hands kneading her breasts now, as flames flickered in her nether regions, her pussy convulsing with need. Oh *God*.

Her mouth opened, panting, as he laced his fingers through her hair and tugged her head back, pulling her ear to his mouth. "I owe you a spanking, young lady. You endangered yourself when you disobeyed me. And because of what you did, you've raised suspicion by plastering your name all over the internet. I don't give a shit who comes after me, but you'll answer for putting yourself on their radar."

She swallowed, her heart racing as her pussy throbbed with need, but at the same time her ass tingled at the memory of his leather on her naked skin, and his enormous hand branding her with punishing strikes. Through the haze of arousal, she looked into his eyes. "And what if I say no?" she said, not able to help herself from pushing, testing, craving his mettle and dominance. "What if I refuse to submit?"

His eyes darkened, his brows drawing together with a startling sternness that made her shiver deliciously. "Refuse to submit?" he asked. "I didn't ask you to submit, little girl. I told you that you were getting a spanking." He frowned, and before she knew what was happening, he stood, holding her, marching toward his bedroom. Her heartbeat kicked up, the heat rising to her cheeks as he marched past the living room to his bedroom. She hadn't seen his bedroom yet, had barely even observed her surroundings, and everything passed by her in a blur now. She needed this. She needed him. And she knew the feeling was mutual.

His room was darkened, the shades drawn, but she could see a large, king-sized four-poster-bed as the focal point, as he marched toward the bed and laid her down on top. "You stay right there, little girl," he ordered, one finger pointing at her. She nodded. Now was not the time to push him, she could tell just by the way he ordered her.

He walked over to a large chest that flanked the foot of the bed, and lifted the top. The air in the room shifted as Blake reached down and removed something from the chest. The tension between them crackled.

I didn't ask you to submit. I told you that you were getting a spanking.

The creak of the chest made her jump, as he lowered the lid and removed a length of rope. She swallowed, hard, as his eyes met hers.

"Strip," he ordered. *"Now."*

I didn't ask you to submit.

Her chin lifted in defiance as her eyes met his and her voice came out clearly and confidently. "Make me."

His eyes narrowed. "I'm not playing games, Elena," he warned. She didn't move.

In two strides he was upon her, yanking her top up and over her head. "So that's how it's gonna be?" he growled, tossing the garment to the floor and making quick work of the bra that already hung loose about her. He grabbed her hips and yanked her toward him, unfastening the button on her jeans, and pulling them down her legs. He tossed her shoes to the side, and after he removed her jeans completely, his thumb hooked onto the edge of her panties, and off they came.

"When you're with me, no panties," he growled. "I check and find them again, we start the night over my knee. You understand me?"

She merely moaned as his thumb and forefinger pinched her nipple, garnering her attention. She nodded, and before she could speak, he'd flipped her over, his broad palm pushing her chest down on the bed, positioning her so that her back arched and her ass was on prominent display. Without further ado, he delivered a sharp, biting slap to her naked backside so hard, the sound resonated in the large room, and she squealed from the sting. "I hope you like my lap," he said, with another sobering slap, "because it's pretty clear to me you'll be spending a hell of a lot of time on it." She moaned as he gave her three more rapid-fire blows. Her skin was already aflame, and she could feel slick arousal between her thighs. Fuck *yeah.*

He moved to the head of the bed, as silky restraints encircled her wrists. "You keep your hands together, palm to palm, and you do not get out of your position," he instructed. "You're getting tied up, Elena, but I'm not wrapping you up the way I'd like, not now, because I want most of your body bared to me." She felt both wrists bound and a slight tug as he expertly maneuvered the restraints. "No need to truss you up when I need access to that ass so I can paint it red. I need to get to that pussy so when I'm done teaching you a lesson you won't forget, I can eat you out until you scream, then fuck you hard so the only thing you remember is the feel of me in you."

Oh *God*, was it possible to come without actually being *touched*? The man knew what the hell he was about, and she fucking loved it.

She could not move her wrists, but it wasn't uncomfortable. She liked the loss of control, knowing that she was the focus of his undivided attention. She pulled her wrists, but as she tugged, the restraints only tightened—not uncomfortably, but strong enough that she knew she wouldn't be able to escape unless he allowed her. He leaned over her, checking the knots, and gave a quick nod she caught from her peripheral vision. "Good girl," he growled. "Just like that, baby. Now before we move onto anything better, you're getting a spanking, young lady."

The sound of his corrective tone, his firm voice, and the fact that she well knew he meant what he said, caused her to shift on the bed. This wasn't for play. She was getting a spanking she deserved. And yeah, the whole room was charged with the exchange of power, her desire mounting, and she'd be willing to bet he was hard as hell as he pushed away from the bed and stood behind her.

But she knew they needed this… both of them.

What else lay hidden in the recesses of his chest, she wondered, as he walked back to the foot of the bed. Would he spank her with a paddle? Cane her? Strap her with leather? She'd had his belt once, and the memory of it had brought her hand between her legs so often she'd lost count. She closed her eyes, willing herself to submit to this. He hadn't asked for her submission, but hell she wanted to give it to him.

The clink of his belt buckle made the breath rush out of her. Her breasts tingled, her pussy throbbed, and her ass clenched at the sound of him pulling it through the loops. A moment later, and the sound of him snapping it behind her made her jump. "Keep your chest down," he said. "Your back arched."

She nodded, then yelped as a stripe landed across both cheeks. The lash of his belt sounded in the small room, like a thunderclap in the silence. She felt the warmth of his hand on her back before another blow fell. The bite of leather on her naked skin burned, her ass aching from the bite, but it wasn't too much, wasn't awful. It was exactly what she needed and craved. As he reared back to strike again, she pushed her ass out to him, silently asking for more.

"When I stripe this ass I want it to be because you need it," he said, "and because I want to, not because you've disobeyed me." The first prickle of her conscience tugged on her, as he continued, peppering his words with sharp cuts of the belt. "I'm not fucking around with this, Elena." Another searing blow. "I want you safe. I want you protected. And fuck me, I don't wanna lose you." The pain in his voice twisted her heart, as she lay on the bed, accepting the punishing blows as due recourse for her actions. "You might think you can handle yourself, and I have no doubt that you can. But I'm here now. You're mine now." Blow after blow fell, and she could feel the rising welts across her backside and thighs as he strapped her soundly. She'd feel this for days. Fuck, she wanted to.

"And I take care of what's mine." She lost count of the lashes, his words drawing the tears out of her, cutting through her proud veneer and straight to her heart. The belt fell to the floor with a soft jingle, and then his hand was on her flaming, aching skin that felt stretched tight from the stripes of his belt. She gasped at the feel of his whiskery mouth on her lower back, a trail of kisses over the heated pain on her backside. "Will you obey me, baby?" he murmured, kissing the swell of her ass, down to her upper thighs. "Or will I have to put you over my knee?"

"Yes," she moaned. Yes, she'd obey him and yes, he'd have to put her over his knee.

He turned her around so that she lay flat on her back, her bound wrists over her head, giving him total access to her full, naked breasts and pussy that fairly throbbed with need. He knelt over her, unfastening the buttons on his shirt while he took her in. "I mean it, Elena. You'll do as you're told. We're new, and I'm easing you into this, but I'm not gonna put up with you endangering yourself. I won't ever strip you of who you are, but I'll also never allow you to half-ass your safety. You get me?"

She nodded. She got him, all right, so fully that she couldn't speak.

His hands grasped the edge of his t-shirt, then he raked it up and over his head, revealing his honed abs, the large expanse of his chest, and massive breadth of his shoulders, before he dropped to his knees in front of her and spread her legs.

Oh *God*.

He took first one leg and then the other, draping them over his shoulders. His eyes met hers. "What'll happen if you're a naughty little girl?" he whispered.

"You'll spank me," she breathed.

He nodded, his eyes meeting hers across the expanse of her naked body as his tongue traced around the edge of her inner thigh, just grazing the edge of her pussy. "With my belt?" he said, the warmth of his breath making her tremble with need.

She swallowed. "With your belt."

Another teasing swirl of his tongue on her inner thigh. "Fuck, little girl, I can taste your juices all the way over here, and I haven't even gotten to where I need to go." He groaned, his eyes closing, and she heard him unzip his jeans, fisting his cock as his mouth latched onto her thigh and sucked. Her hips bucked, her head tossed to the side, and her hands itched to anchor onto his hair, but the restraints prevented her. The tighter she pulled, the harder her pussy throbbed with need.

"I'll put you over my lap," he said, coming closer to where she yearned to feel him, the tip of his tongue torturous but delicious. "I'll spank you hard and long, and any time you need me to. You'll learn to obey. You'll learn to take care of yourself." His tongue slid along her folds. Her pelvis jerked from the sensation, the delightful torment making her yearn for more. He circled her clit before sucking, and her head fell back as she lifted her pelvis closer to him, needing more. His breath fanned her leg, as he breathed, "You'll learn to let me love on you in all the ways you need me to." He licked his way lazily up her slit before circling her clit. One swirl, then another, drawing her into his mouth before releasing and teasing her yet again. "You'll learn to beg."

"Please," she gasped, and he shook his head from side to side, eating at her pussy hungrily, the prickles of his beard scraping along the tender skin between her legs, the bristly sensation enhancing the assault of his tongue on her clit.

He lifted his mouth and growled, "You come before I say, and I'll whip your ass before I jerk myself off while you watch. Then I'll spend the rest of the night bringing you right to the cusp before I stop. You want that?"

"Nooo," she moaned. "Please."

"Beg me," he growled, his hands squeezing her punished ass so that she squealed from the pain of it. "Fucking *beg* me. *I* own this pussy now, and I want you *begging.*"

"Please, Blake, God, *pllleease,* sir. I'll do anything you want. I'll be such a good girl. I need this. Please!"

She moaned, and begged and pleaded, as he sucked and teased, pumping two fingers in her core and finger fucking her while he took her clit in his mouth. She was so close she could hardly hold on much longer, and she knew it, but the idea of being punished again made her somehow able to refrain, to hold herself back, willing herself not to give into the release until he gave her permission.

"Blake," she pleaded. "Let me come!"

He lifted his mouth off her pussy just long enough to look at her, as both hands reached for her nipples and squeezed. The pulse of pleasure-pain shot to her pussy as he grinned at her. "Come for me, baby. Give it to me. Take it." His tongue was on her again, and then she toppled over the edge. Waves of ecstasy pulsed through her, her body writhing beneath the perfect torture of his mouth. A scream sounded in the quiet. She had no control over *anything*, her sex pulsing as he mastered her, her body thrashing, her wrists still bound and helpless, as he rent pleasure from every inch of her. She thought it would never stop, one wave of ecstasy riding on another. Before she was quite done, he was standing, pushing his jeans down, spreading her legs, impaling her with one savage thrust of his cock.

Fuck, he was in so deep she gasped, each stab of his cock rendering her immobile with pleasure. He drove into her with determination, a savage claiming that somehow healed her, making her feel at once both wanted and beautiful. Mastered. Owned. He roared his release as she came a second time, screaming into the dark recesses of the night while he held her close, until they finally settled, both of them, the only sound, her heart beating with his. His hands fumbled at her wrists as he skillfully unfastened the knots, her hands falling open and immediately encircling his neck. He lifted her and fell back upon the pillows, both entangled in a mass of limbs.

"You gonna do as you're told?" he rumbled into her hair, his hand encircling her neck and pulling her possessively against his chest. She nodded, unable to do anything but acquiesce.

"I'll do my best," she said, a compromise that seemed to only amuse him.

"You do your best to do what you're told, and I'll do my best to make sure you do, and we'll be all right, yeah?"

She laughed, her voice sounded deep and sultry to her own ears. "Hell yeah."

CHAPTER 9

"You know this is totally unnecessary, right?" Elena sighed as Blake opened the passenger's side door of his SUV and helped his woman slide down from the high seat, totally appreciating the way the slide made both her skirt *and* her lightweight sweater ride up to reveal tantalizing glimpses of skin. "Driving me everywhere like I'm a celebrity who needs a bodyguard?"

"Yep. And *you* know we already discussed this," Blake reminded her, allowing a warning note to creep into his voice.

Elena sighed again and squirmed just a tiny bit, making Blake grin. Oh, they'd *discussed* it all right, first at his house this morning, and then later when they'd stopped at her apartment so she could change and get ready for lunch with Gretchen. Blake had made it clear, *once again*, that he wasn't screwing around with her safety. When she'd argued, he'd warned her, and when she'd *continued* to fucking argue, he'd put her over his knee and spanked her gorgeous, round ass right there on the edge of her bed, loving the way she'd felt against him, still rosy and naked from her shower. He'd thought he'd been thorough enough to put an end to this conversation for the rest of the morning, at least.

Apparently not.

But it would be his absolute pleasure to rectify that mistake.

He placed his hand firmly on her elbow and guided her to the elevator, his eyes scanning the nearly-empty sub-basement level of the parking lot... just in case. Nothing had suggested that Salazar was planning to up the ante from his harassing protests, but something about the whole situation still didn't sit right with him, and Blake wouldn't take chances.

When they reached the elevator, he jabbed the up button, pleased when the doors immediately whooshed open and no other passengers had appeared.

"Figures. Even elevators obey your will," Elena grumbled.

He turned and speared her with a look that made her eyes widen and her breath come fast.

"W-what's that look for?" she stuttered.

He gave her his most feral smile as he backed her into the empty elevator car. He pressed the button for the top floor, then turned to crowd her against the wall, bracing his hands above her head.

"Look?" he mocked in a whisper against her neck.

"Yes the *'You're in trouble, little girl'* look," she elaborated on a rush, as he ran his tongue over her thudding pulse.

"Oh, *that* look? That look just means I was thinking about you," he said in a low voice, watching the way his breath made gooseflesh rise on her damp skin and just *knowing* that her nipples were hardening beneath her bra.

"Oh... I guess... that's nice," she said, lifting her hands to thread them into his hair.

"Hmmm," he agreed, pressing her more thoroughly into the wall. "Like I've been *thinking* that I've clearly been too easy on you, worrying that you were new to the lifestyle. I'm *thinking* that the next time I spank your ass for arguing and sassing me, I'm gonna have to be a lot more thorough so you'll learn your fucking lesson."

Her eyes widened. "Oh, no, that's not... you don't..."

"Don't worry, baby," he told her. "I take my responsibilities *very* seriously."

He moved one hand from the wall beside her head and squeezed her ass… *hard*… right over a spot he knew would still be tender from the spanking he'd given her an hour before.

She whimpered in a way that was half discomfort, half arousal, and he felt his cock twitch.

Jesus, this girl.

"Now, are we gonna discuss my presence at your lunch date again?" he demanded softly. "Do I need to make myself *any clearer* on this subject?"

She shook her head. "No. I just… didn't want to inconvenience you," she whispered. "I know you're busy, and…"

Blake snorted. "Elena, in just this one morning, you've aroused me, defied me, angered me, and made me laugh my head off. One thing you have *not* done, one thing you *never* do, is inconvenience me. It is my job—my privilege—to take care of you and keep you safe. *That* is my priority. *You* are my priority. Understand?"

His hand soothed the flesh he'd squeezed and she smiled. "Yeah," she breathed.

And damn if that smile didn't communicate itself all the way to his groin.

The elevator dinged open and he snagged her hand, tugging her out into the restaurant lobby. "Let's get this over with," he barked.

He wasn't *just* talking about this lunch, although he couldn't wait to get his woman back to his place, to show her *exactly* how he felt about her sass, and to explore her serious enthusiasm for the Shibari they'd dabbled with last night. He couldn't wait to be done with *all* this bullshit. The protesters. The investigation. The worry for Elena's safety, if these idiots *did* decide to up the ante. The nagging feeling in his gut that he was missing something.

Last night, after Elena had gone to sleep with her head pillowed on his chest, Blake had lain awake for a long while. The last few days had brought him no shortage of shit to think about, from the concern about Elena's possible pregnancy (which, honest to God, had felt more like *hope* than worry), to the quagmire of the protests that were making it nearly impossible to effectively run his business. He'd been running his hands over Elena's soft hair, breathing in the sweet, vanilla scent of her shampoo, when a thought had run across his brain that shocked the hell out of him.

You could just close The Club.

It wasn't the thought of closing The Club that shocked him. Hell, he'd considered it once or twice, especially over the last few years, first when that fucker who called himself Marauder had used The Club to attack Matteo's woman, and again when Josie got sick. Both times, though, he'd dismissed the idea right away. Not only was the place his livelihood, it was his life's work—a place he'd built from the ground up over *decades*. He'd mentored hundreds of dominants, tutored dozens of submissives, and provided a real-life safe place for members of the community, much the way Josie had online. It was more than a business. It was a duty. A *calling*, if you wanted to get dramatic about it.

But last night, feeling the warm weight of his woman pressed against his side, hearing the deep, even sound of her breathing, he found he couldn't give a shit about any of that. It was all about Elena now—protecting her, making a life with her, building a *family* with her.

He dropped his hand from Elena's and placed it on her lower back as he guided her across the elegantly appointed lobby.

He *wouldn't* close The Club unless he absolutely had to, of course, but recognizing that he *could* do it, and walk away without regrets if that's what Elena needed? Yeah, that had helped solidify his priorities. He'd known for a few weeks that he was in *deep* with her. Now he knew he was *all* in.

"Good afternoon," a woman greeted them from behind a podium, distracting Blake from his thoughts. "Welcome to The Skyroom." She appraised Blake from head to toe before tossing him a wide, blatantly flirtatious smile.

Blake raised one eyebrow at her obvious inspection. She was an older woman—his age, or maybe a couple of years younger, short, blonde, and completely lacking in subtlety. Not remotely interesting.

But beneath his hand, he felt Elena's back tense, and saw her eyes narrow as she correctly read the hostess's smile.

Now *that* reaction was interesting.

"How may I help you?" the blonde asked.

Blake deliberately stayed silent, allowing Elena to speak.

"We're meeting a friend for lunch," she said shortly. "Gretchen Liu?"

The blonde gave Elena a perfunctory smile, before returning her gaze to Blake. "Of course. The other members of your party are already seated. If you and your... *daughter* would follow me?"

Daughter. It'd been bound to happen, of course, and Blake was surprised to find that he was more amused than upset by it, especially in this situation. He frowned at the woman severely, waiting for her to realize her mistake.

Not surprisingly, his Elena wasn't that patient.

She tucked herself more firmly into his side, wrapped her arms around his waist, and glanced up at him with a wide smile. "Baby, can you believe she thinks I'm your daughter?" Elena giggled in a high-pitched voice she'd probably never used before in her entire life. "Although it *is* sexy as hell when you call me *young lady*."

Blake turned his frown down at his woman and grasped her hip firmly in warning.

A warning she ignored.

Elena snaked her hand up Blake's abdomen, coming to rest just over his heart. "And I think I'd kinda love to call you Daddy sometimes," she confided in a stage whisper just loud enough to be sure the blonde could hear.

The blonde made a strangled noise, and pinched her lips into a sour pout. "This way," she said, grabbing menus off the podium and sweeping through the open doorway into the restaurant.

Elena went to follow her, but Blake grabbed her arm. "Care to explain yourself?" he asked keeping his voice deceptively mild.

Elena shrugged and looked down, somewhat chagrined. "Just... staking my claim," she said softly, but her tone of voice said she knew she'd crossed a line.

"Uh huh." His hand, hidden from view of the restaurant by the podium, found the curve of her ass and squeezed once more. "You can be certain we'll be discussing that... *later*."

Elena sucked in a breath, then nodded meekly.

Blake turned her towards the dining room and gave her sore posterior a firm swat, but couldn't help adding, "*Young lady.*"

And damn him, but the sight of the blush climbing her cheeks was giving him ideas completely inappropriate for the present moment.

Half pissed off, half amused, and one hundred percent turned on. Was this what the rest of his life would be like, he wondered?

He chuckled to himself.

Yeah, he was *definitely* all in.

He controlled his expression as he followed Elena through the restaurant, preparing himself to meet her friend and talk business, and forcing himself *not* to dwell on the way Elena's shapely legs ate up the floor, or allow the sway of her ass to affect his breathing.

He couldn't fault the choice of location, for sure. The restaurant, which was on the 34th floor of a highrise near Rowe's Wharf, was large and airy, with floor-to-ceiling windows on three sides that allowed the warm spring sunlight to flood the space. The floors were a dark cherry, the linen tablecloths were pristine white, and a panorama of Boston spread out before them in every direction.

They were led to a four-person table in the back corner furthest from the door, where two people were already seated. Blake noted with approval that the man—a guy with the honed physique and sharp eyes of a trained operator—sat facing the room and watched them closely as they approached. The other occupant, a woman with a petite build and hair every bit as straight and black as Elena's own, sat directly across from the man, scowling at him.

"Enjoy your lunch," the blonde told Elena acidly, plunking a pair of menus down at their seats and stalking away.

Both people at the table turned to stare, and then the woman jumped up from her seat with a squeal.

"Oh my gosh!" she cried, her shoulder-length hair swirling around her face as she threw her arms around Elena. "How *are* you, stranger? It's been months and months. Emails and calls just aren't the same!"

While the women exchanged greetings, Blake turned his attention to the man, who had risen to his feet also, consciously mirroring the pose of the woman he was protecting. The guy was easily over six-two, with a lean, muscular build that reminded Blake of Matteo, and the lower half of his face was obscured by a full beard.

"Blake?" the man surmised.

Blake nodded.

"Lucas," the man introduced himself, holding out his hand for Blake to shake.

"You're one of Slay's guys," Blake said, more of a statement than a question.

But the man grinned widely even as he inclined his head. "More like, Slay's one of *us*."

Blake felt his lips turn up. "That an important distinction?"

Lucas shrugged. "We aren't real keen about bowing to anyone else's authority, that's all. Slay's a good guy—when he's leading an operation, he knows I've always got his six. But he's *not* my boss."

Blake nodded, and from the other side of the table, Elena piped up. "We have that in common!" she told Lucas, slinging an arm around her friend's waist. "Alex isn't my boss, either."

Lucas's eyebrows rose.

"Lucas, this is Slay's sister, Elena," Blake said dryly. "You might note the resemblance."

The man smirked behind his beard and gave Blake a look. "I do."

Elena shook the hand Lucas offered, but her brow wrinkled in confusion. "That's funny. Most people don't think we look alike. He's built like Paul Bunyan and I'm... definitely not." She chuckled, taking her seat.

Blake took the seat opposite her. "It's not a *physical* resemblance," he said.

Elena shook her head. "I don't get it."

The woman beside her rolled her eyes. "He's saying you and your brother both have an attitude."

"Oh," Elena said, her face clearing. "Well, *yeah*. But on *him* it's annoying, whereas *my* attitude is adorable."

Gretchen and Lucas laughed. Blake felt his mouth kick up in a smile. "Absolutely, baby."

Gretchen's pretty brown eyes, just a few shades lighter than Elena's, caught Blake's and narrowed, like a hawk who'd caught her prey. "Okay, let's talk about *that*, right there! What exactly is the relationship between the two of you?"

Elena snorted. "Simmer down, G. There's no story to uncover here, okay? Blake and I are together. That's all there is to it."

Her voice sounded confident, but he loved the way her eyes sought his for confirmation.

"Yep," he nodded. "That's all there is to it."

But Gretchen wouldn't be put off. She rolled her eyes again. "Well, *yeah*. We all know that. Heck, the entire broadcast area of Channel 13 Action News and most of YouTube knows that. But what were you doing at The Club in the first place?" She leaned over the table, glancing avidly between Blake and Elena. "How did you get involved in this, Lanie? Are you, you know, his *submissive*?"

Elena glanced at Blake again, this time as though looking for guidance, and felt his temper spike. No one was going to grill his girl on their personal business.

But before he could open his mouth to protest, to draw a firm line around what was off-limits, Lucas spoke up.

"Back off, Vicki Vale," he said airily, earning him a glare from Gretchen.

Blake personally felt that the comparison to the rabidly inquisitive reporter from Batman was pretty apt. So did Elena, if her stifled giggle was any indication.

"Elena is my *friend*," Gretchen shot back. "I care about her and want to make sure she's okay."

"I know you do." Lucas's voice became lower, softer, both a comfort and a caution. "But this is neither the time nor the place for that discussion."

Gretchen darted a glance at Elena, whose cheeks were still pink with embarrassment, and deflated.

"Sorry, honey," she said. "Let's change the subject. Why don't you tell me all about your brother! Is Alex still sex on two legs?"

Elena laughed and relaxed, but Blake noticed that the opposite was true of the man sitting next to him. Lucas seemed to be holding himself very, very still.

Hmmm.

"First of all, *ew*!" Elena said with a smile. "My brother is… enormous and annoying and not remotely hot. And second of all, he's doing great. Remember, I told you in my email that he's been with Allie for about a year and a half, and he's going to be adopting her son, Charlie, any day now?"

"Oh! *Right*! Duh! I forgot," Gretchen said, earning her a curious look from Elena and a glare from Lucas, who'd folded his arms over his chest.

"Seriously? You? *Forgot*? What happened to that steel-trap brain you were so famous for back in college?" Elena teased.

"Good question," Gretchen said ruefully. "My brain seems to have been on hiatus the past few weeks. Don't get me wrong, I'm glad you came to me with this. The guy you asked me to look into is someone I've been hoping to nail for years. A friend of mine had dealings with him and, uh… it didn't end well. My friend's gotten in so deep, he can't get out."

Blake wasn't surprised. Boston was practically crawling with people who hated Chalo Salazar. Unfortunately, the number of people who *feared* him was even higher.

"But next time you ask me to do you a favor, girl, remember I *don't* want protection, okay? I can take care of myself, and I don't need some... some... *professional stalker*... watching my every move and getting all up in my business." Gretchen glowered at Lucas.

Blake bit his cheek to stifle his grin. *Professional stalker.* That was a new one. He glanced across the table at Elena, and saw her eyes widen, no doubt reading the sexual tension that coiled in the air, heavy and potent.

"Hell of a way to talk to the guy who saved your life two days ago," Lucas growled.

"Oh, *please!*" Gretchen retorted, balling her fists on the tabletop. "You didn't *save* me, because I wasn't ever in *danger*, and anyway, I..."

Blake held out a hand, halting whatever else Gretchen planned to say. "How about you tell us what you needed to tell us, and you can sort your own shit later, hmm?"

Fortunately, the waiter showed up at that exact moment to take their orders. Blake and Elena, who had barely had a chance to glance at their menus, ordered basic burgers.

After the waiter departed, Gretchen took a deep breath, visibly forcing herself to calm down and adopt a professional mien.

"I have good news and I have bad news," she began, and Blake felt that knot of tension in his gut tighten once again.

"Start with the bad," Elena said grimly. Consciously or unconsciously, her hand snaked across the table to find his, and he twined their fingers together. Whatever came, they'd handle it together.

"Well, according to my source, you were right on track with your assumption that Salazar is funding The Church of the Highest Prophet. Apparently, he's bragged about it."

Blake nodded. No surprise.

"The bad news is that my source can't get us any *concrete*

evidence. I have no proof of the link between Salazar and the church's effort to discredit The Club. And I won't write unsubstantiated rumors," she said flatly. "Not even for this. I value my integrity too much."

"*Fuck,*" Blake said. Until that moment, he hadn't realized how badly he'd been hoping that Gretchen would have the magic bullet, the one piece of information that would clear up the whole mess for him—and maybe even put away the asshole who'd hurt Slay's Allie, too.

"Yeah," Gretchen agreed with a sympathetic nod. "Let me be clear—it's not that the proof doesn't exist. Salazar is one hundred percent out for retribution, and he's definitely diverted funds through his attorney to the church. He also coerced those women into making false accusations against The Club and filing a civil suit. It's just that it's too risky for my source to confirm this. Salazar would know who'd betrayed him in two seconds flat, and it wouldn't just be my friend on the line, but his family, too."

"I understand," Elena told her, meeting Blake's eyes across the table and squeezing his hand. "We wouldn't want anyone to get hurt."

Blake nodded once, severely. Hell, no. Not on his watch.

"I knew you wouldn't." Gretchen gave Elena a small smile. "There *is* a bright side, though… and it's a pretty unexpected one."

"What's that?" Blake demanded.

"Well, it looks like Salazar has some big plans coming up. My source didn't give me any details, and I sure as hell didn't want to ask, but in my opinion, it sounded like Salazar's tired of hiding in the shadows. He's ready to become a major player in the Boston underground again. Like Voldemort, coming back from the dead." She rolled her eyes.

Blake couldn't see *any* positive light to the news she'd relayed. "What the hell does that mean?" he snarled. "He's gearing up to make a move, and meanwhile my girl got herself on his radar? How's this *good* news?"

Gretchen grinned, not put off in the slightest by his temper. "Whatever Salazar's got planned, he's pulling back all of his resources and gearing up for it. He's all but stopped moving product over the past week, he's had a couple of phone calls that even my source hasn't been privy to, and he's warned his guys not to get so much as a traffic ticket. He doesn't want to be on law enforcement's radar."

"Still not seeing the good news," Elena told her friend.

Gretchen wrinkled her nose. "Well, everyone knows Chalo happens to be *allergic* to publicity. He *never* wants to draw attention to himself, and after Elena's little speech the other night, he's realized that people are starting to connect the dots between him and the protests at The Club. He's decided to cut off cash flow to the church. He's told his guys he's already won—he's succeeded in discrediting The Club, so he can pull his funding from the protests without losing face." She rolled her eyes.

Blake exchanged a glance with Elena, whose jaw was wide with shock... and excitement. He hated to do anything to make her more worried, but the whole thing still wasn't adding up for him.

"Who's your source?" Blake demanded. He couldn't trust the opinion of one of Salazar's cokehead henchmen, not with something as important as Elena's safety.

Gretchen laughed and shot him a disparaging look. "You know how this works. I can't tell you my sources. Once a source believes he or she has been compromised, they generally *cease to be a source*, either because they choose not to risk themselves, or because someone chooses to silence them in a permanent way." She hooked a thumb at Lucas angrily. "A piece of information I *tried* to convey to *this* guy before my last meet, not that it did any good."

Blake looked to Lucas, who merely shrugged. "Not gonna let her meet *alone* with some fucker who works for Salazar," he explained, his thoughts eerily similar to Blake's own.

"And *I* told *you* I don't need your *permission*!" Gretchen all but shouted, drawing the stares of several people at nearby tables.

"You have your job, I have mine," Lucas said stonily. Then he turned to Blake. "But anyway, guy's trustworthy," he confirmed.

Blake blinked. Trustworthy? "Trustworthy" and "works for Chalo Salazar" tended to be mutually exclusive, unless…

"Do I know this guy?" Blake demanded.

Lucas nodded slowly.

Damn. There was only one trustworthy person Blake knew who was affiliated with Salazar. And yeah, he'd believe Diego Santiago's word any day.

"What the hell are you talking about?" Gretchen demanded of them. "You think you know D… I mean, my source? How?"

"I run a BDSM club. I know *a lot* of people, Ms. Liu," Blake said with a shrug and a smile. "So… Your source is sure Salazar will be calling off the dogs? Leaving The Club alone?"

He could see the hesitation on Gretchen's face, and knew she didn't want to be distracted from her original question. He saw her dart a glare at Lucas and didn't envy the man. He was going to be *grilled* the second he and Gretchen left this place.

Lucas, however, seemed unperturbed.

Finally, Gretchen caved and answered Blake's question. "Well, that's the other piece of bad news," she told him. "Salazar's no longer going to be funding the church, which means more than likely they'll be taking whatever donations they have left, locking their doors, and high-tailing it out of town in the dead of night."

She rolled her eyes again and Elena laughed.

"Good riddance," Elena said, and Blake squeezed her hand. *No shit.*

"And he won't be paying his attorney to handle a civil suit against The Club, so that threat will go away, also," Gretchen continued. "But unfortunately, that doesn't solve your PR problem."

Elena frowned. "Why not?"

"Well… The church started the mess, no doubt, but this thing has taken on a life of its own now. You've got online petitions and people setting up protests—"

Blake nodded. "Pandora's box has been opened."

"I'm afraid so," Gretchen agreed. "Unless you really wanted to push the whole Salazar-church connection beyond the veiled reference you made the other night. You might find another reporter who wouldn't mind publishing rumors like that, but…" Her eyes were troubled.

"Absolutely not," Blake declared flatly.

"Right," Gretchen nodded, relieved. "Good. Because if Salazar thought you were going to the media, he *would* come after you then. Elena, too."

Blake heard Elena suck in a deep breath and ran his thumb over her knuckles. "That's *not* gonna happen," he soothed.

Her eyes came to his, caught and held. She nodded, but bit her lip in a way that said she was still thinking about this shit.

Add that to the list of things they'd need to talk about later.

THE LUNCH HAD BEEN PLEASANT, but it had been fucking long. Blake found his mind turning over the issue of Salazar the entire time. He wanted to believe that Diego's information was accurate, and that the danger was past, but knowing Salazar's MO… it just didn't add up. He kept replaying Gretchen's words, sure he'd missed something, but he couldn't put his finger on it.

Once she'd conveyed the information she needed to convey, Gretchen had seemed to relax, and Blake had found her to be sweet and funny… except when it came to Lucas.

Lucas had predictably been quiet, except for the occasional intelligent, wiseass remark, at least until Blake had paid the bill and they'd adjourned to the lobby to say their goodbyes.

Gretchen had shocked the shit out of him by raising up on her tiptoes to press a kiss to his cheek and whisper in his ear, "I'm so glad she's found you." And Elena, in turn, had given Gretchen a big hug and promised to make their lunches a regular monthly thing, at minimum.

But then Gretchen had turned to Lucas and held out her hand. "Well, thanks for your help. It's been nice knowing you," she'd said, trying to be smart, but any idiot could see the genuine regret in her eyes.

Lucas had grasped her hand and lifted one eyebrow. "Appreciate it. But until I'm sure you're safe, doll, I'm not going anywhere."

Gretchen had frowned, completely bewildered, and tried to extricate her hand from his grasp. "Uhhh, *no*. Your job is *done*, my investigation is *closed*, and Blake isn't paying you anymore. You have no reason to stick around."

Lucas had simply smiled and pulled the woman closer to his side to say softly, "I think you and I both know that's not true."

Gretchen had stared at him for a long moment before turning to Blake. "You can… call him off, can't you? Make him go!"

Blake had simply shrugged, amused at the conflicting emotions that flitted across Gretchen's pretty face—joy, wonder, panic. "Sorry, honey. You heard him earlier. He doesn't follow my orders. He's his own boss."

Lucas had snickered. "Come on, babe. Let's discuss this in the car."

"I'm not going anywhere with you," Gretchen had declared staunchly, folding her arms across her chest. "I'm going home."

"You can try," Lucas had agreed. "But remember, I've got your keys."

He'd twirled the keyring around his finger, smiling at the outraged noise Gretchen had made.

"And on that note," Blake had whispered to Elena. "I think *we* should be heading home. We have unfinished business to discuss, too."

Elena had nodded distractedly and allowed him to guide her to the elevator and out to his SUV. But now, twenty minutes later, as they neared the turnoff to his house, she was still lost in thought. It was time to get her refocused.

"Babe, what's up?" he said, reaching over to grab her hand.

"Hmmm?"

"Elena," he said sharply. "What are you thinking about?"

"Oh… nothing," she said, shaking her head as if coming out of a trance. An obvious lie if he'd ever heard one.

"Young lady," he growled as he flicked his blinker on. "It's time we go over some rules."

"Rules?" she repeated dubiously. "Like what?"

"Like, for a start, you don't lie to me. Not ever. Not in the smallest way. If I ask you a question, I want a true and complete answer. Not a *half-truth*, not whatever bullshit you think I wanna hear. *Understood?*"

He glanced at her, saw her face creased in a grimace.

"Yes, of course. I wouldn't *lie* to you," she denied.

"Good. Then, baby, I'm gonna ask you one more time. What's got you so distracted?"

She sucked in a deep breath then blew it out before she replied. "It's not a big deal, just… thinking about Chalo Salazar. About how you have to choose between going after him and implicating him in the protests, or sitting back and letting the protests continue, maybe for *months*."

Blake frowned. "Baby, you heard Gretchen. We go after Salazar in the media, he comes after you."

"And the protests continue," she mumbled.

"So what?" he demanded, pulling into his garage and letting go of her hand so that he could set the car in park and turn off the engine.

"So what? Blake, if we exposed him… if the protesters knew they'd been manipulated from the beginning…" He turned to find her enormous, dark eyes trained up at him. "Then they'd have to leave The Club alone," she whispered.

What the hell? Did she understand what she was suggesting?

"Not gonna happen," he repeated more forcefully, reaching over to unbuckle her belt. "*Ever*. Now get in the house."

"But...The Club!"

"Get in the *house*, Elena. *Now*!" he roared.

"But, Blake..."

Enough of this bullshit. He threw open his own door, and shut it with a resounding *slam* before stalking to the passenger's side and yanking Elena's door open.

"Blake, if you'd just *listen*," she said again, holding out her hands as if to placate him, as if he'd *ever* listen to a suggestion like the one she was making.

He grabbed her around the waist with both hands and hauled her to the edge of the seat, then dipped and slung her over his shoulder.

"Blake!" she screeched. "Omigod!"

He carried her squirming and writhing, to the door that led to his kitchen, unlocked the doors, and carted her through, before delivering a sharp swat right where her ass met her thighs.

"Not another word," he growled as he stalked through the kitchen and down the hall to his bedroom.

He set her on her feet beside the bed and turned to sit on the edge.

"Strip."

She swallowed. And then she obeyed.

Off came the sweater, inch by tantalizing inch, until the garment floated to the floor. She unhooked the skirt, which dropped quickly, puddling at her feet. And then she hesitated.

"Everything, Elena. There's going to be *nothing* between us when I punish you," he told her. "When I *take* you."

She reached behind her and unhooked her lacy blue bra, then slowly drew the straps down her arms and tossed it to the floor, as well.

Shit. The sight of her naked breasts in the afternoon sunlight that seeped through the window was enough to have him momentarily forgetting his purpose. He watched as her nipples furled in the chilly air, saw her hesitate.

"Keep going," he told her, his voice husky with arousal.

She swallowed again, then hooked her thumb into her panties and drew them down her legs.

"Come here," he told her, when she was completely bare, pointing at the floor between his legs.

Without further instruction, she knelt on the floor between his feet and gazed up at him, nervous and eager.

"Usually, when I want to spank that ass, *I* will want to be the one to bare it," he told her, threading his fingers into the hair above her ear. "Because I *own* it, and I like to remind both of us of that." Her eyes burned with arousal at his words, and the sight made his fingers tighten in her hair, the need to claim her riding him hard.

"But today, Elena," he continued, voice tight. "Today, I need you to remember that I own it because *you gave it to me*. Your love is a gift that came out of nowhere during the darkest time of my life, and brought me joy that I never dreamed I'd experience again."

She bit her lip and her eyes flooded with tears that he brushed away with his thumbs. He forced himself to finish.

"You will not risk that. You will not risk *yourself*. You won't even suggest it. Do you understand?"

She nodded.

"Then get over my knee," he demanded.

He guided her up and over his left leg, holding her steady with his left hand on her hip, so that her torso rested on the bed and her beautiful ass was bared to him. He ran his hand over her smooth skin, making her shiver, feeling the corresponding twitch of arousal in his cock.

His girl. His woman. His Elena.

His to protect, to discipline, to pleasure.

Then he lifted his broad palm and brought it down with a resounding *crack* that echoed through the empty room. Elena's answering cry, a muffled sound that spoke of both sorrow and submission, filled something inside of him that defied explanation.

He delivered a dozen more measured smacks in the same fashion, *slap slap slap*, until her entire ass was a delicious, rosy pink, and Elena was writhing against him, her breath coming in short gasps.

"I will never smother you, I will never take away your fire," he told her fervently, punctuating his words with more stinging blows. "But you will *never* jeopardize your safety. That is your first and most important rule."

"Yes, sir," she cried. "Yes, yes, *yes*."

So much enthusiasm while she was over his knee. But he needed to make sure this was a lesson she wouldn't forget the minute this session was over.

"You listen to me, Elena, hear me now," he said, while his palm turned its attention lower, to the tender junction of her seat and thighs. Her back bowed, her torso lifting off the bed in protest with each hard slap, but he would be *sure* she understood. "The *Club* can go to hell. Your *brother* can go to hell. *You* are my priority. Nothing and no one else is worth risking one hair on your head. *Do you understand?*"

He paused, his hand resting on her throbbing flesh, and waited for her answer.

She nodded wildly, her cheek against his bedspread, her hair a tangled mass that covered her face. "I do understand. I promise," she said, her voice thick with tears and remorse. "I understand because… I feel the same way about you. I would never want you to risk yourself, either."

Blake sucked in a sharp breath. His girl. *His*.

"Another thing," he told her, twisting so that he could brush the hair away from her tear-streaked face. "You're mine." He turned her and lifted her off the bed with two hands around her ribcage until she was sitting astride his lap, cradled against his chest. Then he put one finger beneath her chin, making sure her eyes were on him.

"That's not something you have to prove or declare to anyone, ever."

She dragged in a shuddering breath. "Y-your wife. LadyHaven," she began, almost seeming to startle herself with her words.

"Josie," he corrected gently.

"Josie," she repeated. "You loved *her*, too."

Ah. Had this been on her mind? Unlike his concerns about Salazar, this was one worry that was easily banished.

He nodded. "I loved her very much. She taught me so much over the years, baby. She helped me become the man I am now. The man *you need me to be*. And she'll always own a corner of my heart." He stroked his hand over her cheek. "But right now? There's only one person who's on my mind every minute of the day. Only one person who tests my control every minute I'm with her, and makes me crazy every minute we're apart. *My Elena.* My future. I can't tell you how many fantasies I've had of you in this bed. Even before I got my hands on you, I dreamed of you."

"Show me," she said, half plea and half demand.

So he laid back and drew her more firmly atop him, and brought his fantasy to life.

CHAPTER 10

*E*lena glided from the bathroom to the kitchen and then back to her living room, practically floating on air. She'd heard of the whole *subspace* thing, and even had a vague recollection of LadyHaven writing about how after a good, ass-baring, soul-lifting session, she felt like she could sail away, but it had all seemed like some ethereal promise until now.

God, Blake knew what he was doing. She plunked herself on the couch and crossed one ankle over a knee, making the hem of her leggings rise. Running her finger over the delicate space above her ankle, she smiled to herself. The light pink crisscrossed markings were beautiful to her, a secret reminder of the dark foray she and Blake had taken the night before. She could still feel the taut but comfortable way his knots had felt about her, tied across her breasts, past her thighs and around her ankles, trussed up like an offering to him. She'd never been more exhilarated in all her life. And hell, it had been *hot*.

The way he'd focused, his blue eyes fixated on nothing but *her*, as she knelt on his king-sized bed. The anticipation, the way he'd slowly built her arousal with light touches of his hands and mouth, the whispered words in her ear that somehow symbolized everything about him that she loved so much. He was careful and attentive as he tied her, focused and experienced. He was firm yet gentle, and so thoroughly *in charge.*

The spanking he'd given her both chastened and exhilarated, segueing into the most intense lovemaking she and Blake had yet experienced. She'd had no idea that riding him could be so sexy, and had somehow imagined that being submissive to Blake meant she'd always be beneath him as he took her. Had he ever blown *that* theory right out of the water, ordering her to get on top, smacking her thoroughly spanked ass to show her just how to move, grasping her nipples with a growl. His eyes locked onto hers as he ordered her to climax and *fuck* had she ever climaxed. Not one but two earth-shattering orgasms had had her screaming his name as her body gave over to the pain, pleasure, and submission.

God, it was something she'd never forget.

She'd spent the night at his house, then gone back to her own to grab scrubs for work, as he went off to The Club. She'd almost forgotten the man who waited for her downstairs. She snorted to herself. She sorta felt like a celebrity, used to the invasion of privacy. Her own special brand of paparazzi. She'd grown accustomed to being tagged wherever she went.

Her phone rang in her pocket as she grabbed her bag. The second she heard the ring, her heart fluttered in her chest. Would it be Blake? God, she was so head-over-heels for the man. But when she pulled it out, she frowned at the screen. Not Blake. Alex.

"Hey, Alex. What's up?"

"Morning," Alex said. "Listen, I'm not gonna pry, Elena, but I need to know something. Okay?"

She shrugged as she checked her bag for her keys, and zipped it up. "Yeah, okay. What's up?"

"When was the last time you saw Blake?"

Ice began to prickle along her spine as she answered. Of course she'd seen Blake the night before, and Alex would *know* she saw Blake the night before, because all he'd have to do is ask the man tagging them. Though the man on her answered to Blake, Alex was in on their whereabouts.

"This morning," she said. She didn't give a shit what Alex thought. She'd lay it all out. "I spent the night at his place. But why are you asking? You could've just checked with the man you have on me, right?"

"No, Elena," Slay said. His voice was unusually tight, and there was something about it that scared her. She sat down quickly.

"Alex?" she asked. "What's going on?"

"I knew you were with Blake last night," Alex said. "So I didn't bother you. Decided to let you two do your thing. I mean, you're in good hands. But this morning, I was supposed to have a meeting with Blake over coffee, and not only is *he* totally off the radar, but the guy who's supposed to be tagging you is, too."

Her hair stood on end and it seemed suddenly very cold in her apartment as she crept to the front room and lifted the shade. Her voice dropped to a whisper. "What do you mean? I can see him from here. He's in his car. He hasn't left. He followed me when Blake dropped me off, and then Blake went to meet you an hour ago."

Alex swore vehemently. "*Fuck*, Elena. That's not my man. Brian is unreachable. Where the fuck are you?"

"I'm in my apartment," she whispered.

Not Slay's man?

"Stay *there*," Alex growled. "Lock the doors. Do *not* open your doors or leave your apartment. I'm on my way."

The phone went dead. Her hands shook as she put it back in her bag, suddenly feeling as if she'd stepped into some horrible alternate dimension. Her eyes flew to the entryway door in front of her, already dead bolted. She'd done everything Blake said, and--*Blake!*

She took her phone back out and dialed his number, but it only went to voicemail. God, where was he? If the man tagging her was off the radar, that meant the man out front, watching her apartment building, wasn't the man Slay had hired? Oh *God*.

Maybe there'd been an audience when they'd met with Gretchen. *Fuck.*

Stay here? With Blake in danger and one of Salazar's men out there? Fuck *no*. She went back to her kitchen and opened the back door. There was a hallway mutually shared by all, leading down to the basement where the washers and dryers were. The basement door would lead to the back alley where the dumpster and recycling bins stood, and the exit was not visible to anyone in the front of the building.

Not surprisingly, the fifth call she made to Blake went to voicemail, just like all the others. She swore. God, this was all *wrong*. Everything had gone so wrong so fast.

Fuck Salazar and his *fucking* henchmen. She was gonna take this on. She was gonna see who the *fuck* was behind the wheel of that car tagging her. Lifting her chin with grim determination, she marched toward the front of the building to peek around the front, just as Alex's massive SUV pulled up. She heard the click as the doors unlocked, and before she knew what was happening, he was swinging himself out of the truck and marching over to her.

"Get in," he said. She sighed, suddenly realizing that marching over to interrogate a guy packing a weapon and reporting to Salazar was damn stupid.

She hopped up into the cab and shut the door.

"God, you're shit at listening," he said with a growl. "No one's heard from Blake. No one's heard from Brian, the guy who was supposed to be tagging you. And we'll know in exactly thirty seconds when someone starts following *me* who's with you. Thousand bucks says it's Salazar's guy, which means *his* guy found Brian out and that shit's not good."

God!

"Where's Blake?" she whispered.

"Don't know, honey," Slay said. "But we'll find him."

"Damn right we will," Elena said angrily. "And *now*."

Alex gave her a sideways glance, but didn't reply.

"Where are we going?"

"We're getting you to where you're safe, and then I'm tracking down Blake and Brian, *now*." He glanced in the rearview mirror. "Huh. No one following." He focused ahead. "Seems they know my truck."

Alex's phone buzzed, and he hit a button to put it on speaker.

"Yeah?" he growled.

"Slay. You get in touch with Blake yet?"

"No. You?"

The man on the other end of the line swore. "No, man, and just now I heard on the scanner that there was a major car accident on Queensborough. Major, Slay. Looks like there may have been fatalities. We're digging for info now."

Elena froze. "Fatalities?" she said.

"Got Elena with me. Anything you say, you be careful, yeah?"

"Sorry, man. Elena, we don't know who was involved, but that's what we're gonna find out now. Alex, can you take me off speaker? Gotta talk straight."

Alex's eyes went to Elena's before he put the phone up to his ear. "Go."

He shook his head as he gunned the engine and took the road that would take them to The Club.

"Sneaky fucking bastard," Alex growled. "Thanks for the update. You let me know as soon as you get any more news, yeah?"

He hung up. "This shit does *not* get repeated. I'm serious, Elena. You listen to me."

"Fine. Spill, damn it!"

Alex frowned, but began to fill her in. "My inside man confirmed Salazar's men attacked Brian. He was knocked out and cuffed a block away from your place, but otherwise unharmed. No one's found the goon who took out Brian, but there's no doubt Salazar had something nasty planned for you this morning that you narrowly escaped. No one knows what happened to Blake. There was a major car accident right outside The Club, and we're trying to find out now who was involved and if Blake was anywhere near there. My guy will call me when he knows anything else."

God. *Hell.* What had that asshole Salazar done?

Elena felt tears prick her eyes as Alex's phone rang again. Giving her a cautious look, he put it up to his ear. The blood rushing through her head made it hard to focus, and all she could hear was Alex's, "Yeah. Got it. On my way."

He hung up the phone and cleared his throat.

"My guys confirmed Blake's car was involved in the accident, Elena," he said gently, though his jaw was tight, his eyes fixed on the road as he took another turn that would lead them to the hospital. "Blake was injured. No idea what the extent of his injuries were, but we're going now."

The breath rushed out of her and she felt suddenly lightheaded.

"God, it's a damn good thing they didn't come after you," Alex said, his voice pained. "They had one of Salazar's fucking men on you!"

But Elena couldn't even think about her own safety. "We met with Gretchen yesterday afternoon," she said, as Alex drove toward the hospital. "Maybe Salazar knows she's an investigative reporter for *The Star*."

Alex swore.

"Ironically, she told us there was nothing she could do to call Salazar out, because her source couldn't get her proof of Salazar's affiliation with the church without being outed and endangered. But if anyone had seen us with Gretchen, and somehow gotten wires crossed…"

Alex nodded grimly, as they pulled up to the hospital. He was dialing on his phone, But Elena hopped out, not waiting.

"Stay here!" Alex shouted, but Elena was already running. She needed to find out what was going on, and she needed to know *now*. Salazar and his fucking henchmen could go to hell. They'd harmed her man, and this was her turf now. She took the employee entrance, which would grant her access to the emergency room, past locked doors. Though she was a labor and delivery nurse, she'd done a one-year stint in the emergency room a while back, and she knew the layout. Double doors flew open just as she entered the brightly-lit hallway, paramedics running with people on a stretcher.

"Get back!" voices called, and she plastered her back against the wall as the bustle of people ran past her. She craned her neck, eager to catch a glimpse of who lay on the stretchers, but she could see nothing but uniformed paramedics and flashing gleams of the metal poles holding IVs. She was jostled down a hallway and now couldn't see *shit,* which made bile pool in her stomach and the bitter, acrid taste rose to her mouth.

God, she needed to find out what was going on. Doors slammed, and people were *running.* She had to find someone, but as she turned to go to the nursing station, strong arms grabbed her from behind. She opened her mouth to scream, but a large hand covered hers, and she was hauled to an empty room. Frantic, she elbowed her captor, but a deep growl froze her.

"For fuck's sake, stop fighting me," Alex growled. "You're not helping anyone by running in here like a goddamned Florence Nightingale."

She froze, relaxing, as she turned to face her brother.

Alex glared at her. "Blake would kick your ass if he knew that stunt you just pulled. God, Elena, use your fucking head. You think it's wise for you to be running around out there right now? For all we know, Salazar's henchmen are here in flocks. Stay the fuck out of sight until I figure out what's going on."

She looked up at him, and she knew he was right. She stopped struggling, and his brown eyes softened.

"I know you're scared. I know you're a fighter," Alex said, finally releasing her. He swore, shaking his head. "That showdown in Blake's office yesterday, I heard what you said. I knew what you were about, but I thought you were still... I dunno, infatuated or some shit like that." He paused, rubbing a hand across his brow. "But you really do love him, don't you?"

Elena swallowed against the lump rising in her throat. "I do," she whispered. "I've never felt like this about anyone in my life, Alex." She wiped at her eyes. "Please. Let's find out what's going on. I promise I won't go all batshit on them. But I need to know, *now.*"

He looked sternly at her, his jaw working, before he nodded and sighed.

"Let's go."

They walked side-by-side to the nursing station. She recognized Nancy, her friend, and grabbed her arm as she walked past.

"Elena!" Nancy said with surprise. "What's going on, honey?"

"The people they just brought in," she said. "Accident on Queensborough. One was my boyfriend, Nancy. I need to know what's going on."

Nancy's eyes widened. They both knew hospital protocol technically prohibited non-family from being privy to critical information, but Nancy nodded.

"God, I'm sorry, honey," she said. "I'll go find out what's going on, and I'll let you know as soon as I do. Okay?"

"Thank you," Elena whispered.

Alex led her to the waiting room, where she sat in a vinyl-covered chair, waiting for Nancy to return. It seemed like hours, as Alex made call after call. Alice arrived after bringing Charlie to school, followed by Matteo and Hillary, and the small cluster of friends sat in the waiting room, keeping vigil.

When Nancy finally returned, Elena practically ran to her. Nancy's peaked face looked grim, but there was hope in her eyes.

She reached a hand to Elena. "He's injured, and it's bad," she said. "But Elena, he's going to be okay."

Elena closed her eyes, tears pricking her lids as she nodded. "Thank you," she whispered.

Nancy nodded. "Broken ribs, broken arm, serious concussion, but thankfully he was hit on the passenger-side, not the driver's side. He's in surgery now to reset the arm, but he'll be out within a few hours, and I'll take you to him."

Elena nodded, and Nancy took her leave.

Elena turned to face her friends to find Alex standing right by her elbow. "News?" he asked.

Elena took a deep breath and relayed the information Nancy had given her. Alex reached for her hand and squeezed it, as a myriad of emotions swelled up in her. Relief that Blake would be okay. Longing to see him. Fury at Salazar. Annoyance at the protesters.

She took a deep breath, wiping away the tears that had escaped. Blake didn't want her involved. Alex would find a tower and lock her up and throw away the key if she put herself out there again. But no one, *no one*, was gonna come after her man, and she had a card to play that very well could work if everything fell into place. It was time to rally the community.

HOURS LATER, Dom and Heidi had come, bringing trays of food from Tony's restaurant *Cara*. Elena had eaten her fill of chicken parmigiana and hand-rolled ravioli, before everyone but Alex had gone home. Surgery was taking longer than planned, but Elena kept herself busy. She'd logged onto one of the computers in a staff room, accessing the secure network, and as Alex made some more phone calls, she got in touch with the people she needed to. She started off on LadyHaven's blog. LadyHaven had thousands of followers, and some of them were the most prominent members of the local BDSM community. It was an easy matter for Elena to find their online profiles. Within minutes, she was sending off detailed, pointed emails.

Some responses were immediate. Elena could've wept for joy. As she'd relayed her message, she was careful to leave Salazar's name out of it. What mattered at this point was making sure The

Club and Blake were vindicated. And the beauty of her plan was that Blake couldn't get mad at her for putting herself at risk, because she never revealed her personal information.

She began to feel hopeful. Her man would be vindicated. Salazar would be put back into his place. And she wouldn't even get spanked over it.

She grinned, sending a last email just as she heard Nancy in the doorway.

"Elena?"

Elena turned.

"He's ready to see you, honey. Come with me."

AS A NURSE, Elena had seen plenty, and was prepared for the absolute worst when she walked into Blake's room. Though she'd been told the extent of his injuries, she still didn't know what to expect. Alex wordlessly came to her side, and the two of them entered Blake's room together, Nancy holding the door open.

"Company to see you," she said into the room, then quietly took her leave.

Blake's face was paler than usual, but his blue eyes were bright. He sat up when Elena and Alex came in the room. He had an IV attached to one hand, and an arm in a cast, a thin blue hospital gown covering his wrapped chest, and his head bandaged. *God.* Her protective instincts rose and she wanted to *kill* the people responsible for doing this to her man.

Blake grinned when she walked in. "You look ready to tear someone apart," he said. "God, I love that look."

Alex chuckled. "Pretty accurate assessment," he said. "She's got her claws out all right."

Elena frowned, coming to Blake's side, and leaning in to kiss him.

"Of course I do," she said. "I'm not some kinda dumbass who

was born yesterday. I know who did this, and I'm not happy. I'm sick of this shit."

Blake looked to Alex and nodded. "Shut the door and fill me in," he said.

Alex moved to shut the large door, and after it clicked closed, he came and pulled a chair over, indicating for Elena to sit. She shook her head, preferring instead to stand by Blake's side and hold his hand while Alex sat. He leaned forward, his forearms resting on his knees as he addressed Blake.

"This morning, the man on Elena was taken out by one of Salazar's men," he began. Blake swore, sitting up in bed, but Elena tugged his hand to get him to relax, while Alex continued. "Seems Salazar just wanted to make sure Elena didn't interfere, since they didn't harm her. We found Brian today, and he's fine, has no idea what happened. Was knocked out and cuffed, but otherwise uninjured. But meanwhile Salazar's man was tagging Elena."

Elena could feel him stiffen next to her.

"Was?"

"Yeah," Alex responded. "Left when I picked her up."

"I'm fine," Elena protested. "Will you please relax?"

Despite being bandaged and weakened, Blake still managed to fix her with a ferocious look. "Someone pulls this shit and you tell me to relax?"

"Of course I do!" Elena snapped. "You're not helping anyone by getting all upset. You'll raise your blood pressure, and I'll have to medicate you. Now sit back."

Blake narrowed his eyes and shook his head, but his lips quirked up at the edges.

Alex shook his head and blew out a breath. "Better you than me," he muttered. Elena rolled her eyes and made an impatient gesture with her hand.

Alex continued. "So you know I've got inside intel. Salazar's direct orders were to take you out, but make it look like an accident."

Elena's hair stood on end. Fucking *finished?* She'd pull the motherfucker apart, limb by limb. She'd tear him apart with her own bare hands. *God!*

"Elena, sit down," Blake ordered, indicating a second chair.

"I'm fine," Elena protested, but Blake pulled her hand, hard, and waved a finger at the chair. "You look like you're about ready to blow a gasket. Fucking *sit*," he growled.

Alex pushed the chair over so it smacked the back of her legs, making her topple into it in a seated position. She glared. Alex and Blake ignored her, and Alex continued.

"My inside man managed to figure out what the plan was, and he couldn't stop the car accident, but was able to intercept the second man just before it all went down."

"Why the hell couldn't he stop the accident?" Elena asked. "What kinda shit undercover agent is he?"

Blake's hand squeezed hers. She winced, glaring at him. It wasn't fair an injured guy could still be so strong. "What?" she asked. "I shouldn't be concerned about you?"

Blake sighed. Alex addressed Elena. "Elena, if our man blows his cover, he's dead. Got it? Not only that, but we get no inside intel on Salazar. Ever since we got on his radar, things have changed, and we've gotta play it safe."

Alex looked at Blake. "And it looks like Salazar's grudge goes deeper than we thought. It's not just about Gary Levitz going after Allie, or me trying to shut down some of Chalo's dealers. Salazar's been sitting on this for *years*. Looks like Marauder and Salazar were tight. That shit's connected, man. Marauder's Salazar's cousin. Black Box was funded out of Salazar's own pocket, and when Black Box went down and The Club rose to the top, Salazar took it personally."

Blake swore. "When Salazar went quiet after his henchman attacked Alice, I thought he'd moved on."

"Apparently not," Alex said, frowning.

"Marauder. Black Box," Elena said. "That was Hillary, right? The guy who stalked her?"

Blake nodded grimly. "We gave her protection at The Club, but Marauder came after her. Marauder was finally put behind bars, and the negative publicity pretty much guaranteed that Black Box would shut down, but at the time we had no idea how deeply this all ran. Salazar didn't advertise his affiliation with Black Box, even to his men, but now there's too much to hide. That's why Salazar wanted to take down Blake personally, but *also* make sure to discredit The Club."

"What are we gonna do?" Elena asked, her lips set in a line of grim determination.

"We?" Blake asked, his eyebrows rising. "*You're* not doing shit about this."

She yanked her hand away from Blake's and sat back in her chair, crossing her arms over her chest.

"Too late," she said.

It seemed as if the air had gone out of the room. Two pairs of flaming eyes bore into hers as the scary badasses stared her down.

"God almighty," Alex said.

"Spill," Blake ordered.

Elena shrugged. "Didn't mention anything about Salazar," she said. "But, I *did* activate the local BDSM community, and let them know that The Club has been under attack. I did let them know that the most prominent, well-respected dominant in *New England* was in a serious car accident, right after his club was the target of a vicious smear campaign, and I implied it was not accidental. I also happened to notify the wider *online* BDSM community who followed LadyHaven's blog that MisterHaven had been seriously injured in a car accident shortly after his vehement defense of consensual BDSM. I said it was time more of us stood up to defend you."

Elena felt tears prick her eyes. The local BDSM community was a fiercely loyal crowd, and she was proud to be among their ranks.

Blake stared at her, his blue eyes still stormy, but contemplative. Alex pulled out his phone and started scrolling.

"Jesus," he said. "Alice is messaging me. Seems there's a tweet that's gone viral about The Club. Not sure what it is yet, but everyone at The Club knows about what happened to you. Alice says The Club has gotten public support on Twitter and Facebook from around the world. People are talking about staging counter-protests. And they're shutting down all of the haters on social media. Allie says the hashtag #savetheclub is *trending*, whatever that means." He put his phone down. "This is huge, Blake."

Blake worked his jaw, his eyes going from Alex to Elena.

"Slater, give us a minute?" he asked.

Alex got to his feet and nodded. "Yep. I'm gonna call Allie and see what she knows."

The door clicked shut behind him.

Elena faced Blake, her bravado suddenly failing, now that they were alone. Even injured, he was formidable presence.

"I oughta whip your ass," he began, shaking his head from side to side.

"I'd like to see you try with your arm in a cast, old man," she said, standing so she was just out of his reach.

"Go ahead," he said, his eyes twinkling now. "Try to run. You wanna see how fast this old man can move with broken ribs?"

She grinned, pushing her chair away and walking over to him. With his left arm free, he grabbed the back of her hair and pulled her down to him. She squealed, but he held tight, crushing her mouth to his with a ferocity that belied his injuries. When he finally released her, his blue eyes bore into hers, heated and possessive.

"I love you, you brat," he said. "It's gonna be a full time job keeping you in line, but honey, I'm up for the challenge. This is all gonna be okay, baby."

She gently ran a hand along the scruff of his beard, cupping his jaw, before leaning in and kissing him again. "I love you, too," she whispered. "And I'll tell you this, Blake. If you take me on, you won't regret it." She grinned wickedly. "I'll make it worth your while."

He chuckled, making her belly warm and her nose sting.

"MisterHaven tames LanieLove," she whispered.

His eyes crinkled around the edges. "And they lived happily ever after."

EPILOGUE

Regular readers of the this blog will remember that it was two years ago today, on an unusually cold, blustery, gray Saturday in May, that members of this community—dominants and submissives, kink-lovers and quiet practitioners of domestic discipline, those who were regular members of The Club and those who had never set foot in a BDSM club in their entire lives—turned out in force on a quiet Boston street to defend The Club from a band of protesters, and in so doing, reaffirmed every consenting adult's right to love who, when, where, and HOW we choose.

This is a community that holds its privacy sacrosanct, a fact that many groups have used to keep us shamed and powerless in the past. But on that day, hundreds of people from all walks of life were willing to show their faces, to stand up for their truths and refuse to be ashamed. We stood shoulder to shoulder against a group of protesters who claimed to have our best interests at heart, and showed them by our dedication, by our determination, and by our sheer numbers, that practitioners of safe, sane, and consensual BDSM are neither deviants nor victims. I have never been prouder to be a part of this community.

So, on this anniversary, I want to say... THANK YOU. Thank you to those courageous men and women who assembled with us on Queensbor-

ough Street two years ago. Thank you to all of you who could not be with us physically, but were shouting your love and support on social media and on our message boards.

Thank you to all the strong, resilient subs, who know the struggle and the profound beauty of yielding to someone they can trust. Thank you to all the strong, committed, loving dominants who remind us that submission isn't slavery, but freedom.

And thank you from the bottom of my heart to all of you who read my poor attempts at encapsulating the reality of this lifestyle, especially those of you who have taken the time to comment, to share your own stories, and to offer your guidance and friendship. When so many of you encouraged me to take over this blog two years ago, I struggled with the idea. The advice and mentorship LadyHaven gave all of us was irreplaceable, after all, and I could never fill her shoes. But with your kind words and constant support (and, it goes without saying, thanks to the unwavering love and support of my family) we have built this blog into a thriving community—a true haven—that LadyHaven would be proud of.

With love,

Haven's Keeper (aka LanieLove)

"I LOVE IT," Blake told Elena, looking up from the computer screen in Elena's office and clearing his throat against the sudden lump he found there.

"Yeah?" Her voice was equal parts hope and doubt, and he swiveled around in the desk chair to look at her, a slow toe-to-top perusal.

Her toes, painted a pale pink, peeped out from beneath the hem of the dark green robe—*his* robe, to be precise—that swathed her from head to toe and was knotted in a bow just above her waist. Her hair, slightly shorter now than it had been two years ago and damp from her shower, still draped around her like a curtain of black silk. And beneath it, her face, so much more familiar and even more beloved than it had been when they'd started together, was absolutely glowing.

"Yeah, baby," he said, standing and wrapping both arms around her waist. "It's perfect."

He felt her sink against him for just a moment, loving the warmth of her, the absolute perfection of her curves, and the rare opportunity of a quiet moment to enjoy both.

He chuckled to himself, as he reflected on Elena's post and all that had changed in their lives in the past two years. Back then, he'd wanted life to calm down so that he could enjoy his time with Elena. But, to paraphrase the gospel of Mick Jagger, he hadn't gotten what he'd *wanted*, but had gotten what he *needed* instead. His life was busier than ever, and he wouldn't trade one single minute of the chaos.

The Club was thriving after Salazar's attempt to ruin its reputation. In fact, if it wouldn't have meant aiding a known criminal, Blake would probably have paid Chalo for all the free publicity that asshole had scored them. They—Blake, along with Matteo and Slay, who had become partners in The Club, LLC, as of last year—had opened a satellite location on the North Shore nearly eleven months ago that was doing so well, they were in talks to open a second satellite location next year on the South Shore, and possibly promote Donnie to manager.

Salazar, damn his sadistic ass, had not done nearly as well in the intervening years. After all the time he'd spent skating by on his drug, kidnapping, extortion, and racketeering charges, it had been Blake's car accident that had finally, *finally* sent that asshole to prison, at least for a little while. Not on a conspiracy to commit murder charge, much to Elena's displeasure, but for fucking *perjury*.

Seemed Salazar, seeing his opportunity to discredit Blake slipping through his fingers, had moved with haste and without thought when setting up Blake's accident, and had sent his henchman off driving one of Salazar's own, personally-owned-and-registered vehicles. Of course, when Blake had lived to tell the tale--and an eye-witness had given a description and plate number of the car that hit him—Chalo had claimed that his car had been stolen days before. Unfortunately for him, a security camera two blocks away from The Club had recorded Salazar stepping out of the vehicle just minutes before the accident occurred. And the State Police hadn't hesitated to throw the maximum penalty at him—two years in prison for perjury involving a motor vehicle theft.

Blake and his friends had used that time wisely. When the fucker was released from prison in a few more months, Slay and his men had a plan in place to take him down *permanently*.

But they hadn't wasted these years thinking too much about Salazar, either.

Matteo and Hillary had gotten married on a Cape Cod beach nearly two years ago, after Matteo had surprised Hillie with a ring at their daughter Francesca's Christening. They'd moved north of the city, closer to The Club North, which Matteo had overseen from groundbreaking to grand opening, training and mentoring every dungeon master himself. Hillie was still writing—in fact, she'd won some award last year for her books, and Matteo bragged that she was funding their kids' college educations one sex scene at a time. But since she and Matt had given Frankie a little brother, Nico, a few months ago, Hillary was loving the work-at-home mom thing and the flexibility it brought her.

In fact, Hillary's commitment to keeping her schedule flexible and prioritizing her family had been a major influence on Tony and Tess's decision *not* to open a second restaurant, at least not right now. Though *Cara* was a success and had been for years, it was a labor of love for the two of them. The business had been their biggest priority aside from Nora—Tess's younger sister, who'd be graduating from college early and with honors in just a few weeks. Now, though, they were ready to step back slightly, and focus on building a family of their own. Tony had popped the question last Christmas, and Tess was going to be a June bride… and Elena had told Blake in *strictest confidence* a few days ago that they would be wasting no time before trying for their first baby.

Dom and Heidi had been thriving. Dom was some hot-shot at his company, overseeing educational funding for the entire Eastern United States. The financial analysis business Heidi and her friend Paul ran was growing slowly and steadily. Heidi and Dom's son, Rafael, was six months old now, and last year the family had bought a little vacation place—a tiny cabin set on a sprawling, wooded lot up in the middle of nowhere-Maine, where Heidi and Hillary used to go camping as kids. They'd invited all of their group—Matteo and Hillie's family; Paul, his boyfriend John, and their dog Clooney; Tony, Tess, and Nora; Blake's crew; and Slay and Allie's brood—up for a long weekend last summer. It had been an absolute blast, with kids and dogs running everywhere, impromptu baseball games in the field… and some skinny dipping in the lake, while willing babysitters abounded.

Alice was still working towards the college degree she'd started before her son Charlie was born, while pulling a few shifts here-and-there at The Club, and focusing on her growing family. But she'd recently started volunteering with Elena and Nora down at *Centered* and felt like she'd found a new calling working with the young women there. Blake wouldn't be surprised to see her taking a full-time position at *Centered* someday. Slay had kept up his private security work, along with his work at The Club, and had taken on the role of husband and *father* nearly as well as he'd taken on the role of Daddy. In the past two years, he and Allie had had two more sons, in addition to Charlie: Alexander Jr. (known as Lex) and Mason. And Slay made no bones about wanting a fourth, if and when his woman was ready. Seemed like Slay had found *his* calling in populating the world with baby badasses.

Not that Blake was really one to talk, under the circumstances.

Thanks to her role as an unofficial organizer and ambassador for the community, Elena had taken over the running of SubHaven, which had become one of the top-visited lifestyle blogs worldwide, and had made Elena a respected community leader in her own right. Though her bosses at both the hospital and *Centered* had given her nothing but support after her fifteen minutes of YouTube fame, Elena had decided to scale back her time at the hospital, working only one shift per week to keep her certification hours. Instead, she had devoted a good chunk of her time to *Centered*, where she'd raised enough money to endow the new Haven House wing for domestic violence victims that they'd be opening today. But the bulk of Elena's time was spent nurturing her own family.

Their family.

Blake swept his hand up and down his Elena's back and pressed a kiss to her temple before reluctantly stepping back... but his wife wouldn't let him go. She made a groan of protest and grabbed two fistfuls of his t-shirt, while the diamonds on her left hand winked in the sunlight spilling through the window.

"One more minute?" she pleaded.

Blake laughed again, and wrapped his arms around her, even as he warned, "The ribbon-cutting ceremony starts at 2:30. We're leaving here in one hour, *young lady*. If you're not ready, I'm hauling you to *Centered* in this robe. I bet all of the donors and media-types will love it."

"I might be wearing this robe anyway," she muttered, pulling away from his embrace with obvious reluctance, but allowing him to wrap an arm around her and guide her through the connecting door to their bedroom. "It's about the only thing that fits me these days, since I've somehow become part orca."

Blake snorted. "You're crazy, woman. You're no whale. And you know I think pregnancy only makes you hotter." He spun her around so she faced the mirror above their dresser and pressed himself against her from behind. With one strong hand, he gathered her hair back, and laid his mouth against her neck, sucking lightly. He loved the way her head tilted to the side in unconscious invitation—an invitation he accepted gladly.

He quickly sought the tie to her robe and unknotted it, letting his hands rove along her radiant skin. Oh, the things he could do with that tie, if only they had time! But for now, he let it go, and met Elena's eyes in the mirror, watched the heat flare between them, as it always did.

He never took that for granted.

First, he tenderly explored the sensitive curves of her breasts, pulling gently on her swollen nipples. "Look at this," he commanded. "Look at how perfect you are."

Her sharply indrawn breath was the best form of encouragement. He felt his cock strain against his jeans.

He moved his hands lower, over the soft bump that protected their baby. "Look at *this*. My baby, Elena. *Our* baby. Our *daughter*. What could be hotter than seeing you like this? Than knowing that *I* did this to you?"

In the mirror, he saw her eyes glaze over, and watched her teeth bite into her bottom lip.

He moved his hand even lower... found her swollen and wet for him.

Jesus. "And there is nothing sexier than *this*, Elena... knowing this honey is all for me."

She thrust her sweet ass against him, moaning.

God knew, they did not have time for this. Fortunately for both of them, his wife was his favorite hobby and learning her body intimately had been his ultimate goal since the first time he'd bent her over his desk. Also fortunately, they'd had plenty of practice sneaking stolen moments over the last few months. Within minutes, his fingers were sliding through her slick flesh, pumping inside her, bringing her to the edge.

"Come for me, baby," he whispered, his fingers keeping their rhythm while his teeth sank, oh so gently, into her shoulder, knowing that the quick bite of pain would get her where she needed to go.

She fragmented, her back arching, her eyes clamped shut, his name on her lips, and *Jesus*, but she was the most beautiful thing he'd ever seen. His cock was rock-hard just from watching her, from hearing her soft cries.

He moved one hand to clamp around her chest, holding her upright, while his other remained between her soft folds, easing her down from her peak. Then her eyes, bright and hot, opened to meet his in the mirror and he wordlessly bent her forward, bracing her hands on the dresser's edge.

"Hurry," she pled as his hands went to the waistband of his jeans.

Oh, that would not be a problem. After watching her eyes as she went over, he doubted he'd last longer than…

"Raaaaaa!"

Oh, no. No, *fuck*, no.

He stilled with his hand on his fly, and felt Elena tense also. Waiting. Hoping they hadn't heard…

"Raaaaaa!"

Blake closed his eyes and inhaled sharply.

"Your son sounds pissed," Elena said, and his eyes flew open to search hers in the mirror. His narrowed.

"You sound pretty fucking amused by this, Mrs. Coleman," he told her, backing away to allow her to straighten and fumble for the ties to her robe.

"I'm not! I swear I'm not," she said, though her mouth twitched at the corners.

She hurried from the room and came back a moment later, carrying their sniffling son on her hip. His black hair was mussed from sleep, and his dark blue eyes, just like Blake's own, looked seriously pissed off… until they spotted him.

"Da!" the little monster cried gleefully, holding out his arms to Blake.

Blake smiled, despite his annoyance, because he just couldn't help it. He took the baby from Elena, and stood holding them both, one in each arm.

"Asher, my man, we need to have a serious discussion about

cockblocking," he told the baby wryly, ignoring Elena's outraged gasp at his language.

"Clearly, he's not *too* effective at it," she reminded him saucily, patting her belly.

"Hmmm," Blake agreed. "You know, on second thought, don't bother getting dressed. I think I *will* just take you to the ceremony in your bathrobe. And when everyone asks why you're late, I'll tell them how sassy you got—"

Elena snickered. "All right, all right, I'm hurrying," she said. She reached up on tiptoe to press a kiss to his cheek, and run a knuckle over the baby's cheek.

"Wait for me?" she asked.

"Always, baby," he told her, as she ran off to get dressed. Because good things were always worth waiting for.

THE END

JANE HENRY

USA Today bestselling author Jane Henry pens stern but loving alpha heroes, feisty heroines, and emotion-driven happily-ever-afters. She writes what she loves to read: kink with a tender touch. Jane is a hopeless romantic who lives on the East Coast with a houseful of children and her very own Prince Charming.

Don't miss these exciting titles by Jane Henry and Blushing Books!

A Thousand Yesses

Bound to You series
Begin Again, Book 1
Come Back To Me, Book 2
Complete Me, Book 3

Boston Doms Series
By Jane Henry and Maisy Archer
My Dom, Book 1
His Submissive, Book 2
Her Protector, Book 3
His Babygirl, Book 4
His Lady, Book 5
Her Hero, Book 6
My Redemption, Book 7

Anthologies
Hero Undercover

Sunstrokes

Connect with Jane Henry
janehenrywriter.blogspot.com
janehenrywriter@gmail.com

MAISY ARCHER

Maisy is an unabashed book nerd who has been in love with romance since reading her first Julie Garwood novel at the tender age of 12. After a decade as a technical writer, she finally made the leap into writing fiction several years ago and has never looked back. Like her other great loves - coffee, caramel, beach vacations, yoga pants, and her amazing family - her love of words has only continued to grow... in a manner inversely proportional to her love of exercise, house cleaning, and large social gatherings. She loves to hear from fellow romance lovers, and is always on the hunt for her next great read.

Don't miss these exciting titles by Jane Henry and Maisy Archer with Blushing Books!

Boston Doms Series
By Jane Henry and Maisy Archer
My Dom, Book 1
His Submissive, Book 2
Her Protector, Book 3
His Babygirl, Book 4
His Lady, Book 5
Her Hero, Book 6
My Redemption, Book 7

Anthologies
Hero Undercover
Sunstrokes

Connect with Maisy Archer
janeandmaisy.com

BLUSHING BOOKS

Blushing Books is one of the oldest eBook publishers on the web. We've been running websites that publish spanking and BDSM related romance and erotica since 1999, and we have been selling eBooks since 2003. We hope you'll check out our hundreds of offerings at http://www.blushingbooks.com.

CPSIA information can be obtained
at www.ICGtesting.com
Printed in the USA
LVHW051446020320
648714LV00002B/397